THE SEA, THE STARS

TIM MEYER

EVIL EPOCH
PRESS

Published by Evil Epoch Press

Edited by Jenny Adams

Cover Design by Chad Lutzke

ALSO BY TIM MEYER:

Demon Blood Series:

Enlightenment

Gateways

Defiance

Novels:

In the House of Mirrors

The Thin Veil

Less Than Human

Sharkwater Beach

Primal Terra

Lords of the Deep (with Patrick Lacey)

The Switch House

Kill Hill Carnage

Limbs

Dead Daughters

Malignant Summer

Wormwood (with Chad Lutzke)

Pteranodon Canyon

Collections:

Worlds Between My Teeth

Black Star Constellations

THE SEA, THE STARS

TIM MEYER

"On the faraway shores of that strange world, the eyes watched from the distant hollows of the cosmos and the unimaginable depths of the black sea."

Garrett Pryce, *The Sea, the Stars*

ONE

The sounds of the hospital were aplenty, an ambient combination of echoing voices and intermittent chirping of machinery, but the only thing Garrett Pryce could concentrate on was his own bouncing knee. He'd been staring at it for a solid twenty-two minutes when a shadow fell over him, ripping him away from his deep and circling thoughts.

"Mr. Pryce?" the doctor asked. He was a young dude, maybe Garrett's age. Maybe even younger given his smooth, wrinkle-free cheeks and the head of neatly combed-back hair that didn't hold a single strand of gray. He didn't like meeting doctors that looked younger than he was. He didn't like meeting doctors in general, but the younger ones made him feel doubly old, and thirty-six was too young to feel old.

"Yes," he said, rising to meet the doctor's eyes.

"Dr. Brown. Thanks for waiting." Brown extended a hand and Garrett shook it. "First off, your sister is going to be just fine."

Garrett whistled with relief. "That's great news."

"Yes," replied Brown, his eyes studying Garrett's, as if he

knew secrets were hidden behind them, secrets the good doctor wanted to unearth, and if he stared long and hard enough, Garrett's eyes would break and divulge everything.

Not that it was a game, but Garrett felt like he'd won something keeping his face rigid, his secrets hidden. "How is she?"

"Physically? She'll recover just fine. Patching her up as we speak. She's lucky her roommates found her when they did. Otherwise...it'd be hard to say. We might be having an entirely different conversation." He paused and checked his clipboard notes. "Mentally, her spirits are quite good, considering." At this, he raised his attention and studied Garrett more intensely. "Tell me, Mr. Pryce. Was this her first attempt?"

Garrett looked beyond the doctor and down the hall, spotting the room where his sister was being treated. Two nurses were applying bandages to her right wrist. And she...

She was smiling. Laughing as if she'd just finished a joke and her own punchline tickled her just so.

"See," Brown said. "Told you. Her spirits are high. Just finished meeting with the hospital's psychologist and she passed the exam with flying colors." Brown offered a faint smile of his own, an attempt to lighten the mood, but it did nothing to ease the weight off Garrett's shoulders. He didn't know why, but he thought his sister should not be smiling, not even a little bit. She should be hurting, sulking, crying—anything but getting a good chuckle out of this. "Doctor Jameson and I were just curious. Jean told her it was—but was it? Her first serious attempt? Has she ever done anything like this or shown evidence of self-harm?"

Garret wasn't sure he knew how to answer that, not exactly. Not *honestly*. "That I know of—yeah, I mean...there were times in high school when she threatened to do it, you know. When

she was angry at mom or me. I always thought it was for attention or...I dunno...some sort of fucked up defense tactic."

The doctor nodded like he'd heard this story before.

"Never thought she'd *actually* try." Garrett shrugged. "But
things change, I guess. And I haven't exactly been there. My
sister and I...we're not very close. In fact, this is probably the first
time I've seen her in about two years."

Brown lifted his brow in an *Ah, I see* kinda way. "Your sister
gave us a brief family history."

"Did she now?"

"Yes. The two of you lived with your mother who had a
history of drug and alcohol abuse. Sadly, she overdosed and..."

"She died," Garrett finished. He blinked, fending off several
invading memories. *A bathtub. Cold eyes. A funeral that hardly
anyone attended.* Things he didn't care to see right now—or ever,
if he had his way. "She died, summer before my senior year."

Brown gazed at him, still searching for those hidden truths.
Vigilant eyes that tried to drill deep into Garrett's thoughts.
"That must have been hard."

Garrett swallowed the frog in his throat. "It wasn't easy. But
we've dealt with it. At least I have."

"Does Jean have a history with drugs?"

Garrett looked back at his sister again. She was still smiling.
The nurses continued to humor her, laughing along with whatever bullshit anecdote she was telling them.

Garrett felt a hot needle thread up his spine, into his neck.

"No, but again," Garrett said, folding his arms, turning back
to the good doctor, "it's been a while since we've spoken."

"I understand."

"What'll happen to her?"

"Happen to her?"

Garrett bit his lip, pinching the skin until it hurt, then let go. "You know, like, where will she stay? After you're finished with her?"

The doctor looked around as if the question confused him and the answer was scrawled on a nearby wall. "Well, we'll keep her for observation over the next twenty-four to forty-eight hours. After that, we'll discharge her, so long as we determine she's no longer a danger to herself." That amiable smile returned to the good doctor's face, and Garrett wanted to swipe it clean off. "I don't foresee us holding her any longer than that, considering what Doctor Jameson detailed in her notes."

"Discharged?"

"Yes, I'll write a script for outpatient treatment—"

"You can't just release her."

Brown seemed insulted by the adamancy in Garrett's voice. He blinked several times before saying: "And why is that?"

"She needs to be...supervised. Doesn't she?"

"Well, if that's what you think, I suggest you arrange for some supervision."

"I don't have anybody to watch her."

The doctor almost laughed. "I don't mean to sound like a jerk, but that's kind of a *you* problem, Mr. Pryce. Not the hospital's. Of course, *you* could always look after her. Being her big brother and all."

"Me? No—I can't. I'm heading down to the shore this weekend to take care of our uncle's place. He...he passed away recently and left us his house. The place needs to be cleaned out, gutted, and—" Garrett stopped when he noticed the impatient mask on the doctor's face. "Look, I know you don't care, just—I can't deal with this. With *her*. It's too much and I have too much going on. I have a new novel that's due—"

"Mr. Pryce, respectfully. This is an emergency room in a New York City hospital. Not a mental health clinic. I can write a script and have someone get you a list of nearby clinics, but I'm afraid after that...you will have to make the arrangements."

Garrett nodded, his jaw hurting from clenching his teeth too hard. "Yeah, yeah. Okay. I understand. Sorry."

"Now look—I'm not a psychiatrist, but my gut is telling me that Jean didn't *want* to hurt herself today. If she had, then the slice would have been much deeper. You know what I'm trying to say?"

Garrett nodded.

"My unofficial diagnosis, between you and me, is that she's going through a rough patch. Getting her talking to someone and having a professional prescribe the right medication will do a world of good for her. But mostly...I think she needs some time away. From here. From the city. And...someone to talk to. Someone to comfort her, someone to understand her and tell her that everything's going to be all right. Someone to see her through the storm until the clouds clear. Someone who loves her. You know what I mean?"

Garrett didn't respond but his eyes did a pretty good job letting the doc know he understood just fine.

"I'll get those recommendations and that script. You're welcome to stay the night with her."

"Thanks."

As the doctor turned and headed down the hallway, Garrett glanced over at his sister's room. She was looking at him now. Smirking. Waving.

He did everything he could to return the gestures but found he couldn't lift his arm or move his lips.

TWO

The breeze from the open window felt great on her face, and the closer they got to the shore, the more Jean Pryce could smell of the coast. The salty ocean spray filled her nostrils, clearing her nasal passages in such a way that the scent practically traveled behind her eyes and permeated the interior of her skull. As Garrett drove the boulevard, Jean looked out at the dunes temporarily hiding the ocean, and her heart skipped when they passed the gaps between the dunes where the boardwalk led to the sand (which looked like a thick coating of pale peanut butter).

It had been so long since she had felt the sand beneath her toes. They hadn't come out here since they were kids, when their mother used to drop them off for the weekend at their Uncle Jerry's while she went to party and get high with whatever dirtbag boyfriend she was using during that particular stretch of degeneracy.

Jean was looking forward to spending the next week here, reacquainting herself with the shore and all of its majestic offerings. Even though they were nearing the end of September and the island looked more desolate and abandoned than her child-hood memories recalled, she was still excited to be back.

Garrett followed the directions on his phone, cruising the main boulevard and taking the necessary side streets to reach Uncle Jerry's old place. The small summer house (that their uncle lived in year-round) sat at the end of the street and was one side street and two sidewalks away from the beach. The small home hadn't changed much, at least not that she could remember; the pale-yellow, sun-blistered siding still remained. So did the black shutters that flanked every colonial-style window. The brick-bordered concrete patio was there. The single-car garage with a huge dent in the door. The faded roof with a few questionably positioned shingles, the kind that looked like they would blow right off during the next hurricane or tropical storm. Any wind gust over thirty miles per hour would probably do them in.

For a minute the two siblings just sat there, staring at their uncle's place, taking in the labor that awaited them. And that was just the outside. Jean couldn't even imagine the work the inside needed.

"Are we really up for this?" Jean asked.

Garrett remained silent for a spell, seemingly captivated by the memories to which seeing this place again had transported him. Then: "We just have to clean it out. We're not looking to make a million bucks here. Just need to make it sellable."

"Uncle Jerry was a pack rat. I don't know if I even want to look inside." The memories of walking into her uncle's place after their mother dropped them off consisted of towering empty pizza boxes, empty beer cans and dirty clothes on the floor. Receipts, bills, entire months' worth of mail left unopened and scattered around the surfaces of countertops and tables. She remembered counting the bugs she'd seen crawling up the walls and along the bathroom sink. The most she'd counted in one day was fourteen.

She didn't know why she remembered that silly fact. It should have been an inconsequential thing, a thing her mind should have easily forgotten, but being back here shook loose that one little factoid from her memory tree, and that leaf of knowledge had landed perfectly in the forefront of her thoughts.

Fourteen bugs. Creepy-crawly bugs with more legs than she could count. Spiders and roaches, beetles and juicy black ants.

A fury of suggestions attacked her thoughts, all equaling the same notion; they should revisit her earlier proposal and rent a hotel room for the week.

Yeah? Who's paying? Garrett had unkindly asked when she had brought it up the first time. *You? Do you even have a job?*

She'd pleaded with him, informing him of her between-jobs status (mostly true) and that she'd pay him back once she was back on her feet. Or even better—give him a share of her profits after the house sold.

But he'd scoffed at that.

"Shall we?" she asked, trying to sound delighted about the pending assignment.

"Sure," he replied without any enthusiasm whatsoever.

THE INSIDE WASN'T AS bad as Garrett had expected, especially considering how much Uncle Jerry had let the outside go to shit. It was, more or less, what he'd remembered from his childhood; piles of garbage everywhere, but nothing a few days of hard, persistent work couldn't remedy. This wasn't *Hoarders* bad; it wasn't like he needed to call an outside company and have them bring a dumpster or have people in hazmat suits show up and decontaminate the joint. There was work, sure, but his anxiety eased once he saw the relatively harmless condition of the place.

"Shit," he said, moving from the open doorway and into the living room. "This is...manageable."

Jean stepped inside, but not without lingering on the threshold for a beat.

"What is it?" he asked.

She shrugged. "Just...weird. Being back here, I mean."

"Yeah," he said, his eyes darting around the room, locking onto the couch that was home to a few fast-food wrappers, T-shirts and sweatshirts, and even a discarded pair of jeans. The clothes had holes in them, and the jeans had visible paint dots and grease streaks running vertically down the legs.

Classy.

"What did Uncle Jerry do again?" Jean asked. "For work?"

Garrett had to think. "I think he worked on boats or something. Right? That sounds accurate."

Jean made a sour face, letting him know she had no clue, had never kept up on such things, which was why she had asked the question in the first place. "Just tell me this place has hot water." She scurried down the hall and into the house's lone bathroom. Garrett heard the squeak of the shower lever being turned. A few moments dragged by, but, finally, he heard his sister let out a breath of approval. "Thank God," she muttered just loud enough to reach his ears.

"See. Told you. Not as bad as we thought."

Garrett went into the kitchen and checked the fridge. The

second he opened the door a powerful odor that reminded him of sour cottage cheese and bad hotdog meat hit him at once. He almost barfed upon experiencing that awful combo but saved himself by shutting the door immediately and turning his entire body in the opposite direction.

"Holy shit," he said, coughing, hoping the Wawa sandwich he'd devoured earlier wasn't about to pay his mouth another visit.

"What is it?"

"The fucking fridge."

"What's wrong with it?"

Garrett waited for his stomach to settle before telling her, "Don't open it unless you want to lose your lunch and possibly the dinner you haven't eaten yet."

She seemed to accept this suggestion as a challenge. Slowly, she turned for the fridge.

"Don't do it, Jean."

But it was too late; she already had her hand on the handle and was pulling open the door. She took in a quick whiff, then closed the door. "Okay, that was nasty. What was that? Spoiled cheese? Meat?"

"I have no idea but stop talking about it. I'm gonna fucking hurl."

"Go outside. Get some fresh air. It'll help."

He nodded, thinking he should do exactly that. And quick.

"I'll handle the fridge," she told him. "Nothing I can't stomach. I worked as a school janitor a few years back. This is nothing compared to what I had to clean up there. You wouldn't believe how many kids miss the toilet when pooping. High school kids. Isn't that weird?"

Garrett didn't speak another word, fearing that opening his mouth would summon forth the vomit.

He did as his sister suggested and headed outside, taking in all the fresh ocean air his lungs would allow.

ONCE SHE HAD FINISHED WINDEXING the fridge's shelves, she took the clothespin off her nose and headed to the front door, taking the trash bag filled with all the expired and rotting contents along for the walk. Stepping outside into the bright sunshine, she found her brother sitting on the porch, hunched over with his head not far from his knees.

"Gonna be okay, cowboy?" She couldn't pass on the opportunity to harass him. It was the sisterly thing to do. "No shame in puking."

"I'll be fine."

"Great. Be a doll and bring this to the curb then." She dropped the bag on the concrete porch a few feet away from his hunched form.

He squinted at her against the sun. Then he pushed himself to his feet with the strength of a hobbled person.

He did as she asked, bringing the garbage to the curb and plopping it on the pebbled strip between the property and the street. Then he shuffled back to the porch.

She folded her arms and enjoyed every second of his miserable trek.

THREE

Hours later, Garrett felt more up to the task of cleaning out the place. But before he got down to business, there was the matter of setting up his laptop and answering a few emails, specifically the messages his agent kept sending him about the impending deadline for his new novel, *Killing Spaces.* The pitch had already sold to Random House, and they were expecting the manuscript by the first of the following month but...

He hadn't written a single word of it.

Garrett didn't believe in writer's block. Never had. After the smooth sailing of cranking out that first work, *Flowers in the Garden of Death,* a dark crime novel that had received some very high praise and starred reviews in some very important periodicals, he didn't believe he could fail at writing another one. Didn't believe there would be a day when the words just wouldn't come. However, the sophomore experience was far different from his freshman outing and, so far, the only thing he had to show for his effort was two words—the goddamn title.

He'd done everything the same as he had when he had pumped out that first novel, every routine and inspirational habit down to a T. But every time he sat in front of the laptop to plow through a few thousand words, his mind went blank, and his fingers seized like some arthritic plague had taken them hostage.

But this week felt different. It was a return to his childhood, a moment in time where he could revisit and access old memories, and he hoped that would rouse the creative force within him, the right mindset needed for *Killing Spaces*. It was another dark crime novel, but this one had a slight coming-of-age bend, and he thought being back here where he had spent so many summers would help him tap into that source where all the great words came from, and the not-so-great words too. That creative well all artists drew from.

He fired up the laptop and cleared out his emails. There were a few messages from fans that said nice things about *Flowers*, and he starred some of them so he could respond later, when he had more time. The email he knew was waiting for him was on top, and he opened it immediately. It was from Joel Harris, his agent, and the subject simply read: *How's it going?*

He didn't want to let the inquiry go unanswered for too long; Joel was a nervous guy and the fact that Garrett hadn't turned in a single word, let alone a chapter or two, had put him on edge. He thought about telling him the truth and begging Joel to ask the publisher for an extension, but he was new to the business and didn't want to disappoint anyone, especially Joel, the superstar agent who'd taken a chance on *Flowers* when no one else would and had actually sold the fucking thing. The advance—compensation that was practically unheard of in publishing today—wasn't much, but it was *something*, and the book was selling surprisingly well, enough for Garret to quit his day job teaching high school English.

He simply replied to the email: *It's going! I'll have news soon.*

He hit send without rereading it, not allowing himself the chance to add something he'd later regret. Promises he couldn't keep.

I'll get it done, he thought. *I'll have it started by the end of the week, and once I get going, there'll be no stopping me.*

Just like last time.

He had serious doubts about producing a full ninety-thousand-word manuscript over the next thirty-plus days, but, if he had *something* to turn in, there was a good chance Joel could get him an extension.

But he had to do it.

He had to put in the work.

Doubt circled his thoughts, and even writing that terse email felt like a minor struggle.

Garrett sighed, closed his laptop.

It was time to work on something else. It was time to deal with the past, the memories of this place.

The good and the bad.

JEAN DIDN'T KNOW WHY, but the painting on the wall over the couch called to her. There was something cool about the acrylic piece that summoned her from across the room and demanded her attention. Uncle Jerry wasn't the artsy type, and she was surprised that he had something that looked like it cost more than what he could afford from a garage sale. In her vast professional career (of working too many dead-end jobs to count), one of them had been with an art museum in Brooklyn.

She wasn't the artsy type either and was surprised how much some of those paintings went for. The one hanging above Uncle Jerry's couch looked more like the ones she had helped sort and hang in the gallery a few years back.

The painting was of a dark and angry sea, a bolt of lightning crashing on the horizon. Arching, whitecapped waves bobbing on an obsidian surface. A fishing boat caught in a wild storm; the sails being blown by furious gales. Two fishermen stood on the deck beneath gray, violent skies, observing the chaos at hand. Jean squinted, staring at one of them, who looked—oddly enough—like their Uncle Jerry. The fisherman was wearing a yellow rain jacket, but it was the scraggly white-gray beard and gaunt face that caught her attention, making her realize the peculiar resemblance. The other was dressed similarly; his beard was just as long but snow white.

"Are you ready?" Garrett asked from behind her, pulling her out of the scene.

She turned to him. "Yeah. Where do we start?"

Garrett nodded over his left shoulder. "The bedrooms are pretty fucked. Lots of stuff in there. Figure we can sift through them first."

"How's your stomach?"

"Better."

"Good." She looked back at the painting, an unsettling chill sweeping through her, leaving her bones numb and tingly.

"You okay?" asked Garrett.

"Fine."

"We don't have to jump right into it, you know." Garrett swallowed as if he was about to broach an uncomfortable topic, one better left alone. "You can rest. I know it's been a strange and tumultuous week."

"I'm fine. Really."

"Okay then." He nodded at the kitchen. "There are some garbage bags on the counter. Bring them and I'll start going through the closets. We'll get them cleaned out first."

Jean nodded, watched him go.

As she went to the kitchen, she couldn't shake the feeling that the painting had eyes and they were watching her.

———

THE CLOSET WAS STACKED with shit. Literally garbage. Food wrappers and shipping boxes, along with items that looked like they'd be rejected by even the most desperate thrift shop, were piled high. There was so much stuff in there it pushed against the sliding doors, forcing them off the track. Garrett put his hands on his hips, sighed, and then turned to Jean, who sat on the edge of the bed holding out an open garbage bag.

"This is gonna suck," he noted.

She agreed, knowing it was going to suck big time, that this whole project would. But they had the whole day ahead of them, and if they could get through the closets, that would be a huge win and a sizable dent in their week-long workload.

"Better get to it, big brother," she said, winking.

He got on his knees and started throwing stuff over his head. She picked up the things that were obviously trash and put them in the bag. The things that were questionable, things they might want to keep or give to Goodwill or sell on eBay, went in a separate pile. There wasn't much of the latter, and by the time Garrett had cleared out a space wide enough for him to crawl into, she'd already filled three thirty-two-gallon bags.

Once in the closet, his back half hanging out, Garrett moved into a downward dog position and began scooping the trash between his legs like some canine digging a backyard hole. "The fuck?" he said about two minutes into the dig. He paused for several seconds, then continued to rifle through the junk, no longer hustling and carefully handling whatever he'd laid eyes on.

"What is it?" Jean tried to look around him, but she couldn't see anything past his body and the door save for the Hawaiian shirts hanging above him.

Her brother didn't answer. Instead, he audibly struggled— growling and grunting—with some unknown object, as if he were excavating it from the earth. After a few moments, he emerged with the object in question.

"What the hell is that?" Jean asked, staring at what had caused the stoppage. It was a stupid question because she knew damn well what it was. What she meant to ask was—*why the hell is that thing in Uncle Jerry's closet and where did it come from?*

A treasure chest the size of a deluxe handbag rested between Garrett's knees. He sat cross-legged on the carpet, keeping the thing on his lap. It looked grimy, centuries old, and it gave off a moldy, sour smell, one she suspected the two of them should not be inhaling due to its potentially toxic nature. Behind that lovely scent, the salty bite of the deep sea tainted the air. The chest's latch was corroded beyond repair, and the lock keeping it shut was just as rusted. Jean feared she might catch tetanus just from staring at it too long. She almost begged Garrett not to touch it when he ran his fingers across the barnacle-covered hood.

"It's a chest," Garrett said, unable to lift his gaze from the object.

"I know that, silly ass. But where did it come from?"

Garrett sniffed the wooden exterior, the dull, lacquered finish. "I don't know. But it smells like a pirate's taint."

"Gross, dude."

Garrett chuckled at his own jest, something he did often, something Jean might have made fun of him for had she not found the mysterious chest so captivating.

In the aftermath of the lame joke, he continued to inspect the chest, shaking it and examining the lock, pulling on the corroded and crusted metal with quick, forceful jerks in hopes the thing would give, pop loose and unveil the mysteries within. But nothing happened and the lock held.

Jean's curious gaze traveled over its wooden surface. Something about it comforted her. She couldn't understand why that was; there was nothing special about the thing that could have come from the set of a *Pirates of the Caribbean* movie, nothing at all. It was an antique, sure, but Jean had never been into old things, especially when it came to décor. She was a contemporary girl, through and through. The apartment she rented with a few friends (the temporary room she could barely afford) was modernized, free from the styles of the last few decades. In fact, anything with an 80's or 90's aesthetic bothered her on some basic level, shows and movies included. And this…even though it wasn't necessarily anything that would become the center-piece of any mantle, still had the feeling of something that had been in style decades ago, longer.

Centuries.

She shouldn't have liked it.

But her eyes could not leave the pitted metal lock, the potential secrets this little wooden box might be holding inside.

Then…she heard something. Someone speaking. No, not

just *one* voice. Many of them. They were low, whispering, like an autumnal breeze kicking leaves across a concrete sidewalk. They were barely present, in the background of her thoughts, her mind, but distant.

At first.

Then they began to rise, get louder, and even though she couldn't make out what the voices were saying, *the whispers,* she knew they were present and there were more than a few, maybe more than a dozen, and they were speaking to no one else but her, and she could—

"Jean," Garrett said sharply, tearing her eyes away from the chest, forcing her to look at him. His voice suggested this wasn't the first time he had called for her attention, and, considering the way he tilted his head, it was probably not the second time either. Or third.

How could she have ignored him when she was only a few feet away?

"Where'd you go?"

"Sorry," she said immediately, even though losing herself in her own head was hardly something to apologize for. She had liked being there, in that moment. It had felt good.

Felt right.

"You were staring off," Garrett explained. "Like, really focused on this thing. And you were...I dunno. Looking at it like a hungry cartoon character. You were practically licking your lips and slobbering."

"Shut up." Dramatically, she rolled her eyes in a *oh-stop-being-silly* sort of way.

"I'm serious." He shook his head as if her little mind adventure disappointed him in some way. Then he rose to his feet, treasure chest tucked under his arm. After he stood, he gave the chest a little shake. Something rattled inside. "Wonder if there's anything valuable in there."

Jean shrugged. "Let's open it."

"Well, it requires a key." He set the thing on the dresser and then tugged on the lock, pulling it with force, trying to muscle what he thought might be brittle metal, weakened by a long stretch of time and the salt of the sea. "Nope, that's not gonna do it." He glanced around the room, scanning the *maybe* pile that Jean had culled from the trash, and then located his desired target. "Ah, there it is."

He picked up a hammer with a cherry-red handle from under the heap. It looked fairly new in comparison to everything else Uncle Jerry had left behind, no wear and tear on its gleaming metal head. Bouncing the business end in his other hand, he turned to the chest and said, "Let's do this."

The first strike landed true but did nothing to pop the lock. The rusted piece did its job and held together. The second, which Garrett brought down with more force, also failed to free the shackle. The locking mechanism stayed intact, and Garrett's third attempt was also refused, the metal hammer making perfect contact, sounding brutish but failing to free the desired secret within.

Denied, Garrett took a step back and sulked in the aftermath of his failed effort.

"Let me try," Jean said, peering at him with those little sister eyes, the gentle, innocent gaze she used to use when she wanted to play football with him and his friends in the park after school.

"Jean..."

"What?" Her nostrils flared as she pursed her lips. "Let me guess—I'm too weak, you're stronger, 'If I can't do it, what makes you think you can?' Right? Tell me I'm right, Garrett. Go ahead.

Tell me I'm a girl and I can't possibly do what you can't. I'm listening. Say it."

Garrett cleared his throat. "I was...uh, just going to say—I didn't want you to strain your muscle and pop the stitches in your wrist."

"Oh," she said, folding her arms, keeping the bandage part hidden. "Sure you were."

His shoulders rose and he arched back, staring at the ceiling for a beat, as if that would somehow clear his mind. "Okay. You want to give it a whack, I won't stop you."

"You won't?"

"Nope."

"Okay." She pushed herself off the bed, strolled across the room, and grabbed the hammer from him. Then she turned, placed the hammer's head on the lock in preparation for the strike, then raised the tool over her head with both hands.

The whispers. Calling her.

She ignored them, their quiet cacophony, and brought the hammer down squarely on the metal lock. There was a tremendous click, a noise that indicated something had broken, but when she inspected the position of the lock, she saw it had not budged, cracked, or moved in any way. It held firm, together, a robust guardian of her uncle's secrets.

"Good try," Garrett told her, the easy sound of his voice attempting to placate her, a gesture she did not appreciate. "You gave it a good—"

Without preparing, she went in for seconds, bringing the hammer down with force, smashing the lock with all her might. The impact did nothing, though the violent act, the ferocity of her movement, felt good. It was a release of something ill that had been trapped inside her, the same kind of emotional purge going to a spa or getting a massage or sitting for a mani/pedi often accomplished. Something escaped her, something she'd been holding onto for a long, long time, and for far too long. The third strike made her feel even better, even though it did nothing to break the goddamn lock, that devoted bastard.

A fourth strike.

A fifth. The lock held like it was the first time.

A sixth.

A seventh.

No luck.

An eighth attempt with more rage behind her now, the movement savage and seeking the ultimate destruction, a level of wrath Jean Pryce had never explored before.

But the lock remained an uncrackable nut.

The ninth and—

"Okay, okay, that's enough," Garrett said, snatching the hammer out of her hands as she reached the highest peak of the tool's ascent.

The whispers in her head died some.

Some.

But not all.

Slowly they left her. One by one, fleeing silently, dissolving into the great dark void where ghostly memories were often kept.

"WE SHOULD JUST TOSS IT OUT," Garrett told her, placing the treasure chest on the kitchen counter. "I mean, there can't be anything valuable inside."

"How do you know? There could be gold or, like, I dunno—a million dollars or something."

"Because I doubt Uncle Jerry kept a million dollars in the bottom of his closet. You remember him? He'd spend entire days taking a metal detector to every square inch of beach, hoping to find a couple of quarters. He wouldn't let something valuable sit like this."

Jean continued to stare at the chest, somewhat vacantly. The wooden box seemed to absorb her childlike gaze, trapping her in that inert state. "But how do you know for sure? Maybe he couldn't open it either. Maybe he never knew what was inside of it."

"Come on," Garrett said, suppressing a laugh. "You don't really believe that; do you? Uncle Jerry would have dropped this off a skyscraper just to find out what was inside. You know that. Mom always said Grandma used to call him Curious George. You remember the stories?"

Jean didn't seem like she cared to revisit one of their mother's or grandmother's Uncle Jerry stories. "Maybe. But I like it. There's something about it...I want to keep it."

"It's going in the trash. Smells weird as fuck and I don't like it."

Jean pressed him with her eyes. She kept needling him with her gaze, waiting to see if the look alone was enough to budge him on the decision.

But it wasn't. He held. He hated the thing—for more than a few reasons, none of which he could adequately articulate at the moment. It gave him a vibe, the kind only a hot shower and a new bar of soap could help cleanse, but even that, he felt, would not eradicate the feeling this small object had laid on him.

"I'm tossing it," he finally said, trotting out his authoritative tone.

On the way to the front door and through it, he felt Jean's gaze follow him, burning a hole in his neck.

He ignored it. Brought the chest to the bottom of the drive and plopped the stinky wooden piece of shit on the small pile of trash bags that had already accumulated. Wiping his hands on his shirt, as if ridding himself of any potential germs, he spun back toward the beach house.

A woman stood no more than twenty feet from him, parked at the end of the neighboring driveway. Her tight curls of gray hair fell around her shoulders, and they blew softly in the autumn breeze. She folded her hands in front of her stomach, flashing him a welcoming smile.

"Geez," he said, placing a hand over his heart. "Scared the hell out of me, lady."

Her face morphed into one of instant regret. "Oh my, I'm so sorry. I didn't mean to, honest. I..." She rotated back to the house next door, signaling the place with a noncommittal wave. "My name is Patti and I live next door. Saw you out here and I just wanted to introduce myself. Never even saw a for-sale sign go up. Are you two the new neighbors?"

He watched the woman flick her eyes toward Uncle Jerry's front door. Garrett quarter-turned to see Jean making her way out onto the porch while looking slightly confused.

He faced Patti again and said, "Oh, no. Not really. Well, for a little bit. Our uncle owned the place and we're just staying the week to help clean up and get it ready for—"

Patti gasped. "You're Jerry's nephew!"

Garrett nodded, scratching his neck. "Yep, that's me."

The woman beheld Jean, realization sparkling in her eyes. "And you're his niece?"

Jean smirked, possibly admiring the woman's quirky introduction, or enjoying watching her brother squirm in this awkward social situation. "Yes, ma'am," she replied.

"Well, golly be. Heard so much about you folks! Say, ain't one of you a fancy, famous writer type?"

Garrett heard a giggle escape his sister. "Yes, that would be me," he admitted. "Not famous, though. Or fancy. I've only written one novel. It's gotten some good praise and it's entered a fourth printing, which is really good considering it's only been out for about six months. Anyway, I'm working on another one and—"

"Your uncle was really proud of you when that book came out," she said, her tone changing slightly, taking a darker, more somber turn.

"He...was?"

"Oh boy, was he. He wouldn't shut up about that damn book when it came out. All he did was talk, talk, talk about your book and how we should all read it. Well, at least, that's what he told me and my husband. Said he'd get us signed copies, but he never made good on that promise. Your uncle...sometimes he said things he didn't really mean. He—" She gasped and immediately covered her mouth as if she had caught herself uttering devilish words best left unspoken. "Listen to me, speaking ill of the dead. Shame on me."

"Oh no, don't worry about—"

She waggled her forefinger, cutting him off at once. "No, no. That is my mistake. Your Uncle Jerry was a good man. A *great* man, and I shouldn't be going on about him like I just did."

"Well...apology accepted." Garrett showed her a toothy smile. "But honestly—it's no big deal. Think nothing of it."

This brought the warmness back to her face, her smile. "You're a nice boy, Garrett. I can tell."

"Well, thank you. I guess."

Jean was giggling again behind him. He'd hear about this exchange later. She'd use this to rag on him the entire week.

"I was so sorry to hear about your uncle," Patti continued, taking turns between facing Garrett and Jean, making sure to relay her sorrow through wet, blinky eyes and a pouty lower lip. "Drowning in the ocean." She clicked her tongue like she disapproved of him leaving the world this way. "Such a terrible way to go. And he was so young too..."

"Well, our family is cursed, so, it happens."

"Why on Earth would you say a thing like that?" She stared at him, her expression wiped clean, and Garrett couldn't tell if the question was rhetorical or not.

The longer the silence built up between them, the more he thought he should elaborate. "I was just...you know—kidding."

"Death isn't something we kid about here, Mr. Pryce."

"Please, call me Garrett. And I'm sorry. My sister and I—we've been through a lot. Not sure if Jerry told you about us or how well you knew him. But our family...we're kind of...well, shit. Our father passed when we were young, and my mother—Jerry's sister—raised us. Alone. And she, um..."

"He told us," Patti admitted.

"Yeah, well, sometimes we kid about things, things we probably shouldn't. Helps us, I think. Gallows humor, y'know?"

Patti continued to study him. Then, her face broke into a forgiving smile. "Everyone grieves differently. I understand."

"Exactly."

"Well, you two should get settled in. I won't take up any more of your time. If you'd like, I can bring by some fresh catch later. My husband goes fishing every morning and today was an especially good one. Lots of tasty treats. It's almost as if the ocean knew you two were coming!"

Garrett twisted back to his sister, then faced Patti again, unable to hide his sourness at the mention of eating fish. "We're not big seafood people."

"No? Well, golly. Maybe you haven't eaten the right kind?"

"Yeah, maybe." He tried to remain positive on the outside, but inside his stomach turned at the thought of sticking something that came from the sea into his mouth. "But we're more burger, hot dog, sub sandwich kind of people."

"Hmm. Noted." She tapped her forehead like she was storing this information in the vault of her mind. A peculiar thing, but then again, everything about this conversation had been a little off. It wasn't that Garrett disliked the woman—how could he? He'd only known her for all of five minutes and she seemed nice enough. Nice, but also...

Weird.

But then again, the island's lifers were all a little strange. He thought back to their childhood when he'd spend weeks at a time with their Uncle Jerry, meeting all types of new people. How they all acted a little strange, different from the city people he was used to. Uncle Jerry himself hadn't been the epitome of normal either, so, it was accepted that people out here just acted a little differently.

Patti spun back to her house and began walking the short way up the path. "Hope you two enjoy your stay in Tripp's Isle. I'll be next door if you need anything."

Garrett waved, watching her disappear up the small walk

that was eventually overtaken by dune willows that flanked either side of the path a few steps before meeting the woman's porch.

Then he turned and faced his sister. Jean was chuckling behind her hand, and he knew he'd never hear the end of this.

FOUR

Jean stared at the sandwiches on the table in front of her, wondering if sandwiches were the only thing on the menu this coming week. Garrett dug right in, stuffing his mouth full of the ham and cheese hoagie.

"Do you remember my buddy Steve from high school?" he asked, lettuce falling from the sandwich, landing on the paper plate. A splat of mayonnaise followed.

She squinted, trying to recall. "Shottenheimer or Riggle?"

"Shotty," he said in a manner that suggested she should have known.

"Uh, yeah. He had the lazy, floaty eye thing, right?"

Garrett nodded, low-key.

"The one who tried to fuck me at your graduation party?"

Garrett cringed. "Yeahhhh. That's him. He's a real estate agent now. In lower Manhattan. Still—he thinks we can get two-fifty for this place. At least."

Jean scanned the joint, wondering where those dollars were hidden. "Really?"

"Yeah, apparently shore houses are going off right now. He has clients splurging like crazy on summer homes."

"Huh." Stomach growling, she stared at the sandwich. She removed the top slice of bread and began picking at the toppings. Shoving a tomato slice in her mouth, she felt her anxiety heighten. Her wrist itched something awful, and she forced herself to resist picking at it. In that moment, she wanted nothing more than to rip off the bandage and start scratching. "Garrett?"

"Hmm?" His mouth was full of sandwich, his cheeks swollen with ham and cheese, lettuce and tomato, and an unhealthy spread of mayo.

"Do you think something's wrong with me?"

He placed the sandwich on the plate as if it were easily breakable glassware.

"Like," she continued, feeling the need to elaborate, "like there was something wrong with Mom?"

"What do you mean?"

"You know what I mean."

He chewed what was in his mouth, swallowed it, then wiped the corners of his mouth on a napkin square. "Mom had issues."

"I have issues."

"Mom had *deep* psychological issues. And a really bad drug problem. She used to smoke meth right in front of us. Remember?" His shoulders slouched some. "Look, are you on drugs?"

"Just what the doctor prescribes."

"See. You're already better off than she was. Mom never wanted to get help. She tried to beat her demons all on her own. You remember how stubborn she was. Refused to see a doctor or psychologist, refused to go to rehab." He sighed, seemingly bored with this conversation. "You're not like her, not at all."

"I'm serious, Garrett. Sometimes I feel good. Normal. *Great*, even. Happy. Not a thing bothers me, and then—sometimes it's like, out of nowhere, I feel really low. Like the lowest of lows. Like, I'm trying to breathe underwater and there's nothing but water in my lungs. And then my thoughts, they turn on me, and I feel like hurting myself is the only way I can feel better again."

Garrett slumped in his seat. "Jean maybe now isn't the best time to talk about it. Not over dinner."

Jean shrunk, feeling less like an adult, more like a kid again. Being told to keep quiet and eat the vegetables or no dessert for you. "Oh, okay. Would you rather talk about our neighbor and how she totally wants to fuck you?"

The question caught him off guard. "Huh?"

Jean rested the side of her head on her hands, pouting her lip and batting her eyelashes. *"Oh, Garrett, you big famous writer man you!"*

"Shut up," he said, going back to his meal, stretching his lips around the ham and cheese hoagie, his teeth sinking into the soft, bready shell.

"Patti totally wants to jump your bones, dude."

"Shut up," he said again, suppressing a laugh.

"Seriously. You should get on that. Maybe that's your problem, why you're wound so tight. You just need to get laid."

Garrett stopped midchew. "I don't have a problem. I don't have any problems." His eyes slimmed to slits, and Jean knew she'd struck a chord. "And I certainly don't have *that* problem."

"Oh yeah? When's the last time then?"

Now he almost choked on the bread-heavy mouthful. Somehow, he was able to swallow and breathe at the same time. "I'm not having this conversation with you."

"Why not?"

"Because. We're eating. And it's...inappropriate."

"Inappropriate because we're eating, or inappropriate because you're talking to *me*."

"Both."

"Why?"

Garrett glowered at her. "You're my sister. It's weird."

"Come on. We haven't spoken in years, Gar. We're practically strangers here. Two strangers, just having a conversation about our lives."

"Even weirder then."

"You can talk to me about things." She leaned forward as she bunched her lips, muscles constricting, stopping the flow of all the things she wanted to say. *Just open up, Garrett,* she thought. *Just talk to me. Please?*

"Not about that."

"Fine. What *do* you want to talk about?"

He placed the sandwich back on the paper plate. "Must we always be talking about something?"

"You don't like me very much, do you?"

"Jean. That's an awful thing to say. Of course, I like you."

"You *do* think I'm like Mom, though." She regretted the words the second she had spoken them, but they were out there now and she couldn't take them back, not *those* words. Those words were immovable.

"That's...not true."

"Yes, it is. You don't even see me as a sister, do you? You see me as a problem. Just another one of life's little inconveniences you have to deal with along the way to...wherever it is you want to go." She felt her upper lip writhe. Her neck ran hot, a flash of heat that felt like a bad sunburn. "I saw the way you were talking to the doctor back at the hospital."

Garrett lowered his gaze, unable to make eye contact. She knew the next words out of his mouth would be a lie, but she listened anyway, hoping he'd avoid being the same old Garrett she'd always known. "Jean...it's not like that. I..."

"Yeah, right." She shook her head. "You left when Mom got bad. You left when she was at her worst."

"I went to school," he told her, as if that excuse solved everything, wrapped up the whole saga in a nice little bow. "I had to go. I got offered a grant—what was I gonna do?"

"You left *me* alone with her."

"Jean, I'm sorry. I thought we went through all of this, years ago. Why are you bringing it up now?"

Jean pushed the potato chips around the edge of her plate. The fire within continued to burn through her veins. "Maybe I am like her, you know? Maybe you're going to leave me too."

"Jean, I'm not leaving you. I'm here. Besides..." It was his turn to lean forward. He tapped the table with his fingers, signaling the next words were the most important of the evening. "You're not like her. Not at all. You understand?"

The fire in her veins simmered some, her anger melting away.

"Do you feel responsible?" she asked. "For mom's death, do you think..."

She watched him chew on his inner cheek. "No. No, I don't."

The fact he said "No" twice made her think he was lying. Like, saying the word twice was a way to convince *himself* it was true.

"Jean, if I knew what was going to happen, how things would have played out...I never would have left."

But how could he not have known? *She* knew, and she had always assumed he was better at *knowing* than she had been. That he could read people better, situations. Which was what made him a writer. A good one.

Liars make good writers too, said a voice, one she almost recognized too. *Liars make the best writers.*

"You have to believe me," he told her.

She didn't. Believe him or have to.

"But regardless," he continued, picking at the bread of his hoagie, still unable to focus directly on her, "I should have been there. I shouldn't have left, and you're right—it wasn't fair to you. I was selfish. I just wanted what was best for me, and I didn't....didn't even consider you or how you felt, how me leaving would affect you."

She digested this apology, this admission, and then nodded. It was the first genuine thing he'd said all night. Since he'd shown up at the hospital. "Okay."

"I can make it up to you."

She rolled her eyes, shook her head. "And how are you going to do that?"

He sat back in his chair, seeming to kick around a few ideas. Then, the faintest grin pushed his lips to the outer edges of his face. "Let's start with a joke."

"A joke? Are you serious?"

"Sure. Jokes have serious healing power. You didn't know that?"

She closed her eyes, deciding to let it go. For now. It was going to be a long week, and it was best not to press her brother too much on the first night. "I do like a good joke."

"Perfect. Then..." That grin stretched a mite farther. "Do you know what the ocean told the sand?"

She tried to think of the punchline, guess before he could deliver it, but gave up after ten seconds.

"Nothing," he said. "It just waved."

"Wow. That is...that is way dumber than I imagined it would be."

Garrett's trademark chuckle rose from the depths of his throat. "Come on. It's funny. Admit it."

"I will admit no such thing."

They exchanged awkward smiles, the pre-joke mood still lingering like unwanted houseguests.

Garrett broke the silence first. "Look, I fucked up. I wasn't there for you, for Mom, when you both needed me the most. But I'm here now and I'm not going anywhere. Got it?"

A tear leaked down her cheek. She nodded, brushing away the salty drop with the back of her forefinger.

Before she could respond, forceful knuckles raged against the front door.

GARRETT WAS ALREADY on edge from their conversation. He didn't like it, not a bit, and least of all, he didn't like the not-so-low-key accusation of abandoning his sister all those years back, leaving her alone to deal with the mess that was their mother.

But that's what you did? Didn't you?

He didn't care for his own personal commentary either, but he couldn't shut it off, so he was glad when someone knocked on the front door, though, at this hour, nothing good could possibly be waiting on the other side of it.

This hour of knocking was reserved for bad news.

Garrett faced his sister. Jean arched her brow. She mouthed, *Well?*

He didn't want to be the one to answer it. He wanted to wait until the knocker got the hint and fucked off back to wherever they'd come from.

What if someone is in trouble?

Garrett peered over his shoulder once again, fixing on the door, waiting for another attempt.

No knock came.

He pushed himself to his feet, abandoning his half-eaten hoagie, and strolled over to the door, allowing his feet to land softly on the carpet, hoping to keep quiet and not alert their mysterious visitor, should they be waiting on the other side with a weapon, ready to club or shoot him the moment he opened the door. He'd seen way too many home-invasion flicks to think of any other scenario.

Garrett sighed, found his spine, and then gripped the doorknob. Opening the door, he found the porch vacated, not a single shred of evidence that someone had been there. He was surprised and relieved all at once.

Just as he began to assume the knock had come from a bored neighborhood kid on a doorbell-and-ditch dare, he glanced at an object near his feet, no bigger than a package that would fit neatly in the mailbox. Upon closer examination, he realized it *was* a package of sorts, a folded square of butcher paper tightly wrapped in thin plastic. A faint, fishy odor wafted up from it, tickling his nostrils and turning his stomach, making him revisit that nasty, rotten-fridge smell from earlier. Luckily this odor wasn't as bold, and he was in no danger of losing the hoagie he'd scarfed down.

Garrett crouched, picked up the gift with both hands. He didn't know what compelled him to do so, but he brought the offering inside, had no clue why he placed the package on the kitchen counter rather than just tossing the thing in the outdoor trashcan.

"What is it?" Jean asked, peering over his shoulder and down at the gift.

"I don't know."

"Should we open it?"

Garrett felt they should, even though every bone in his body leaned toward, *Throw the fucking thing away you fucking idiot.*

Still, his curiosity was thirsty. And opening the gift was the only thing to quench it. "Give me a knife."

Jean dug through the utensil drawer. She produced a fork. "No knives."

He forgot he'd gone through the drawers and culled the knives earlier, removing scissors and anything else he'd deemed too sharp, threw them out with the first bag of trash they'd taken from the first bedroom.

"It'll work," he said, taking the fork. He pronged the plastic, shredding through it with relative ease. Once open, he folded back the butcher's paper to reveal the contents within.

The odor rising up from the food (could it be called that?) was intense, sharper than the smell the fridge had sealed in, but not as vomit-inducing. There was almost a freshness to the stench that one might find alluring, but Garrett (and his disinterest in all things seafood related) didn't find the stuff appetizing in the least.

"That's…" Garrett said, taking one step back as if that would knock down the odor's bite. "…interesting."

"It looks like," Jean said, leaning forward, having a closer look, "caviar?"

He wanted to warn Jean, tell her not to get too close, that the thing looked more like some alien *goo,* not something sickos put on their sushi rolls or crackers or whatever else caviar was used for.

This wasn't caviar. He was sure of it. Small, shimmering black globules sat on the center of the butcher's paper, resting in a shallow puddle of dark juices. They did look like miniature eggs or fish roe, the small pile enough to toy with Garrett's gag reflex.

"I might actually hurl," he admitted, his eyes tearing as the smell intensified. This was the opposite of most unpleasant odors —the stench seemed to be gaining power rather than staying stagnant and giving his nose the opportunity to acclimate.

"You're such a baby." Jean crumpled the paper into a tight ball and transitioned the gift to the nearby garbage can.

Garrett watched the stuff drop inside and immediately experienced a warm rush of relief. Like he'd just dodged something dangerous.

Death.

"You know what," Garrett said, raising his forefinger in the air, the way Mom used to when she was about to make a point, a valid one. "I'm going to shit on her porch."

Jean blinked rapidly and shook her head. "Excuse me?"

"That woman. Patti. I'm going to march over to her house and take a big steaming dump right on her goddamn porch."

"That's…what? Why?"

"Because she left that shit on ours," he stated, like this was obvious news. "She asked us if we wanted any fish, remember? 'Fresh catch' was the exact term, I believe."

"You're losing it," Jean said. "Maybe I should be chaperoning you."

"I'm serious. I can crank out a couple turds and then we'll call it even."

"The fact that I think you're dead serious about this is very concerning." She shook her head. "I feel like you need to talk to someone."

He couldn't tell if she was joking or not.

"Besides," she continued, "how do you even know it was her who left it?"

"Who else would it be?"

"Some kid?"

"Some kid?" He *tsked* her. "Come on. You honestly think that?"

"It's late. I don't know what to think. But taking a shit on someone's porch is crazy in every sense." She nodded in the direction of the back bedrooms. "I think we should get some sleep. It's been a weird first day."

He contemplated not giving up and marching over to Patti's place, giving her a piece of his mind. Not shitting on her porch— Jean was probably right about that one—although he didn't rule it out. But as the seconds passed, he calmed down and realized how childish he was being.

"You're right, you're right." He shook his head, finally giving himself over to the notion that Jean was the level-headed one in this situation. It was late. He was tired. And he wasn't thinking clearly.

It has been a weird day, he thought. *Too many memories of this place, too many unwanted thoughts.*

He took what was left of the sandwich and placed it in the trash, letting the ingredients rain over the mysterious dark substance that had been left on the porch. Not wanting the stuff to linger in the house any longer than it already had, he took out the trash immediately.

Out there, on the side of the house where the black trash-cans were stationed, he turned toward the beach and swore he saw pale torchlight flickering somewhere on the other side of the dunes.

FIVE

Jean couldn't remember every detail of the dream, not exactly, but she remembered this: a black ocean that stretched for miles beyond her eyesight, her swimming the fathomless water's ominous lengths, a destination unknown even to the dreamer. A gibbous moon, brighter than any she'd ever seen, left a streaked, luminous path for her to follow. She swam in that shimmering trail, gliding through the liquid fantasy with ease, propelling herself as if she were of some amphibious design.

Then, the dream went sideways. There was mostly black, an encroaching shadow that enveloped the setting, folding over her and plunging her into an inky, cold realm. She couldn't feel the cold on her skin—this dream wasn't immersive like that. Instead, it felt more like a presence emerging from within her own body, another *her* extricating herself from flesh, muscle, and bone. A frosty unease replaced that new, nonexistent part of her.

Then she woke up. Sweating, her skin clammy. Heart beating like the wings of some maddened butterfly. Walls of impenetrable darkness all around her, the clock on the nightstand only providing a sliver of light with its green, digital numbers glowing and blinking.

There was a brief moment of absolute silence where she heard and felt nothing, but that moment passed shortly after and the whispers flooded her ears, a thousand faceless voices luring her along, begging her to step through the open doorway and down the hall.

Outside.

Beyond.

A blink later and she was outside, standing on the pebbled pathway that wrapped along the side of the house, sifting through the trash, following the whispers and their whimsical demands.

She was hungry after all. Starving, in fact.

She scooped up handfuls of discarded refuse, shuffled through them looking for that particular package, the one Garrett had tossed out earlier that evening. Once her fingers gripped the plastic, she felt some unspecified power surge through her, like bolts of lightning dancing through her veins. In seconds, the butcher's paper was before her, sheared open, and she was staring at the juicy black contents of this unknowable substance.

Sharp pangs of hunger needled her stomach. The need to eat, and that primal instinct flowed through her, making it impossible to think about anything else other than devouring what lay before her.

She couldn't resist.

Dipping her fingers into the sludgy, ocean-born substance, she licked her lips, her mouth filling with water. She loaded her fingers with a small mouthful of the egglike feed, then brought her fingers to her mouth where her lips had parted, and her tongue was reaching out to meet her hand halfway. The food of unknown origin, sticky and sweet and surprisingly tasty, swished around her mouth, hitting her taste buds in all the right places, imbuing her with a sense of comfort and inner peace. In that moment, nothing else mattered. Not the arduous, impending task of cleaning out Uncle Jerry's place, not her recent brush with death, the one she'd brought upon herself because she had felt trapped in her own head, a space that was supposed to feel safe and secure and wholly hers but where negativity—that tyrannical monster—ruled the kingdom of her thoughts.

She swallowed. It was in her now, that *unknown thing.*

Her fingers returned to the dark, nutritious well before her. She had seconds. Thirds. Before she knew it, the small heap of tarlike clumps was gone, traveling through her system, and all that remained on the paper was a shallow puddle of glossy black. Of course, she drank it. All of it. Every drop. She opened her gullet and poured it down until the plastic was clean and the forbidden fruits of the sea were gone.

The whispers were at peace but still present.

They spoke tirelessly about the beach, the black waters. The secrets that lay just beyond it.

The Sea, the Stars, they said.

And it sounded like music.

GARRETT ALSO WOKE up from a dream, except he remembered nothing. He stared into the darkened corners of the room, the only light coming in through the window via the moon. The blinds were open, and the moon threw luminous slits onto the bed near Garrett's feet.

He could have gone back to bed. A bone-deep exhaustion plagued his body, and the toll the last couple of days had taken on his mental state had set him up for a successful sleeping experience, but there was a quality to the night that pestered him, and it was as if his body roused him for a specific reason.

Jean?

He swung his feet off the bed and shoved them into his slippers. As he made for the door, a sour but bitter taste teetered in the back of his mouth. Swallowing that along with any hesitations, Garrett poked his head into the spare bedroom where his sister was sleeping. Or...

Had been.

"Jean?" he asked the emptiness, the shadows. The shadows did not reply. He flicked on the lights and found the bed empty, the sheets crumpled, lying in a pattern of endless wrinkles.

To say Garrett panicked wasn't entirely accurate. His heart danced funny, jigged in a way it never had before, but his nerves, the way they burned like someone had set them aflame, were what truly concerned him. It felt as if he'd gripped fistfuls of hot, exposed wires and fried every molecule his body contained.

He turned from the bedroom and headed for the kitchen, hoping to find his sister raiding the fridge (though, what was there to raid—nothing) and stuffing her face full of midnight snacks. But the kitchen was dark and also belonged to the shadows.

"Jean?" he said, finding his way through the lightless area, bumping into almost every single obstacle he could—a chair, the garbage can, the counter. He opened the fridge door just to let the light escape. Then he located the light switch, flipped on the row of recessed floods above the sink, and hoped Jean had taken to the couch in the living room. Or, at the very least, he hoped to discover that she was still inside the house.

But...*nope.*

The front door was open, letting a late-night draft into the room, an early-autumn chill that permeated everything including Garrett Pryce's soul.

"Oh no," he said audibly, though he'd only thought those two words.

Oh no indeed.

Jean was gone.

———

JEAN MARCHED ACROSS THE NIGHT. She went where the whispers directed her, meeting their demands and feeling good about it. Feeling *right.* Like she belonged to them and they to her. Even though she could not hear what they were saying exactly, could not make out specific words and phrases other than, *The Sea, the Stars,* she followed their voices in the direction she thought they were speaking from. At first she had assumed the voices were only inside her head, just another symptom of her constant unease, her daily anxieties, or the depression that sometimes felt like it was just too much to handle, too much for her body and soul to defeat. That this was one more sign to confirm she was, in fact, a crazy person. A nut like her mother, sans the excessive drug and alcohol use.

But I'm not crazy, she thought, heading over the dunes and down the beach, where obsidian waves lapped at the shore. Moonlight like smashed glitter sparkled on the surface, giving visibility to the tide, the choppiness of it all. At first she had thought this was her destination. That the sea was inviting her into its depths with open arms, but as she neared the fanning water of the crashed waves and the wet sand beneath its touch, she realized that wasn't where the whispers were steering her. There were other treasures to discover, to behold.

Secrets in the dark...

She spun in the direction of the pier, the wooden structure that was wider than it was long. The pier extended out over the water about the same distance that ran from the dunes to the ocean. A small amusement park had been built atop it, and, in the dark, Jean could make out the Ferris Wheel, an arcade, a carousel, and a candy shoppe that announced it had the best saltwater taffy on the shore. *Guaranteed!*

These were dark places now. A month ago, this area might have been alive, even at midnight, but now, off-season, only the dark ruled this hour. Jean drifted toward the pier, the absolute black that held the spaces beneath, pockets of impenetrable darkness that stood like hellish portals leading to some subterranean nowhere.

Despite her misgivings, Jean closed the gap between her and that inky wall.

Closer, she was able to make out a figure standing just outside the entrance to this hidden labyrinth. Hooded and robed in equally black attire, the figure stood still but beckoned her forth with a long, arching finger, its complexion one with the moon.

Jean didn't know why but she smiled.

Suddenly, through all this darkness, the world seemed a little bit brighter.

"JEAN!"

Garrett rushed down the dune, nearly slipping and falling onto his back. His ass touched the dune's decline, but he bounced right back to his feet like one of those inflatable punching clowns. Assuming the footprints in the sand belonged to her, he was hot on his sister's trail. He followed the tracks to the shoreline, watching the waves crash on the wet sand and fan out in great foamy arcs. The darkness of the ocean and the incredible night above it ensnared his attention. Midnight stars speckled the sky, some of them blinking like weak flashlights on low batteries.

He shook his head, escaping from the vastness of it all. Then he glanced down, examining the direction of (hopefully) Jean's path of travel. He craned his head and caught sight of the pier in the distance, the cavernous dark beneath its robust structure. On the pier's surface, a Ferris Wheel, along with a group of tents and shoppes, stood like some relic of times long since passed, derelict and cursed to remain so forever.

A sudden movement captured his eye, and Garrett focused on the pier's dark underneath, crisscrossed with beams and girders. Below them, a single figure traveled toward that black portal, drifting dreamily toward a hungry void.

"Jean!" he cried out the second he kicked his legs into a furious sprint. Garrett tore down the sand, his muscles aching after the first few strides. He hadn't endured this much physical activity since...when? College? High school? Even back in the day during gym class he'd always been the kid to hang out next to the bleachers, avoiding the teacher's probing eye. He hadn't run this hard since he had tried out for the soccer team in inter-mediate school.

But...he pushed through the burn, the slight pain under his ribs, accelerating across the sand and ignoring the waves crashing against his ankles, soaking his shoes. The wet sand made it easier to run on, and he continued to push himself until he was standing under the shadow of the pier, the uncertain area where the moonlight could not reach. Where the pier's secrets were kept, deep and dark and down.

Jean was gone, though. She had left behind footprints that disappeared into the impenetrable abyss before him.

He made a cone with his hands, placed them over his mouth and yelled, "Jean!"

No answer, not that he had expected one. Truth was, he didn't know what to expect. This...this wasn't like her.

Well, what do you know? Not like you been around lately.

His mother's words. Her *exact* words. She'd said that to him once, when he had visited her and Jean at some point during his sophomore year at college. Mom had been in one of her infamous moods—drunk and sloppy and slurring every other word—and Garrett had had the talk with her, the one he'd had multiple times before, but this time he'd been more forceful. Sat her in the chair and told it to her straight, *no bullshit* as she would say if the roles were reversed. *"Mom, you need help. Like now. Get up. I'm taking you somewhere."*

Garrett had always assumed she wasn't fully listening because her only response was, *Well, what do you know? Not like you been around lately.* And then had proceeded to kick him out, flinging a beer bottle at his head. When that didn't drive him out of the apartment, she had smashed a whole bottle of cheap whiskey on the floor near his feet. Told him to, *Get the fuck out and never show your face again.* Which she added would be payment enough for the broken whiskey bottle.

He had listened. To the first half of her request. As far as never showing his face again...he had. Only, that next visit was the day his mother died.

Garrett stared into the dark void before him, his mom's final words to him echoing through the chasm of his mind. He opened his mouth to call his sister one more time, to tell her she needed to come out right this second or...

Or what?

What could he do?

Nothing, he determined. Took about twenty seconds to decide the only way to get Jean out was to go in after her.

THE CHEST GLOWED NEON GREEN, pulsating and electric, and with it, the secret whispers rose, damaging the silence.

Lots of things were currently fuzzy in her mind—like how she had gotten here, how the chest ended up in the sand before her. How the key to the padlock had mysteriously appeared between her fingers. It all felt like part of the same dream she'd woken up from prior to her nightmare stroll across the beach.

Maybe she never woke up. Maybe she was still there, deep in the depths of her dreaming mind. Maybe it was the kind of dream one could never wake from.

Maybe she was dead and this was Hell and she was—

She slipped the key into the lock and listened to the satisfying click as the mechanism disengaged. Her hands acted on their own, sliding the shackle through the chest's latch hole, freeing it. Lifting the hood, she glued her eyes to the glow within. Once her vision adjusted to the throbbing light, she saw what rested there.

A conch. No bigger than her iPad. Harmless enough. Just a shell, a beautiful-looking ornament with a spiked spire on one end and a flare-lipped opening—almost ear-like—on its belly.

Just a conch. That's all it was.

She held it with both hands, staring into the dark slit where she thought she saw something moving, something cautiously probing the exit. The once pulsating light had dulled now, and the shadows returned, crawling back over her, the moonlight unable to reach this far under the pier. Her eyes did their best to adjust to the night, but the grainy dark was not forgiving. She made out the outline of the conch, most of its distinguishable features, but everything else was drenched in the inky filth that covered this place.

The whispers gave her unsolicited advice, their partnered chirping, a disharmonious chorus she felt compelled to sing along with.

She whispered with them, her lips moving at a frenzied pace, trying to keep up. Deep in the whispers, she heard their demand and Jean knew she'd have to comply. She'd follow their lead because she knew she couldn't refuse.

They wouldn't let her.

Just like they asked, she brought the conch to her lips and tilted back her head. From the conch's slit, a dark fluid leaked out, like melted candlewax losing the fight against gravity. Jean stuck out her tongue, ready to accept the offering. A single drop landed on her taste buds; a taste so sweet that when she swished it around her mouth, a sharp bite like a papercut blossomed along her lower gumline. She grimaced, trying to ignore the sudden pain, and continued to drink, placing her lips on the source and allowing the dark donation to fill her cheeks to their maximum capacity. Then, in one big gulp, she opened her throat and swallowed.

A rush of euphoria collapsed over her like one of the ocean's fierce waves. A tingly touch grazed her arms, the back of her neck, numbing her senses.

She wiped her lips and glanced at the midnight smear on her arm, her wrist.

The whispers were back, louder than ever. They buzzed like a bog full of chatty insects.

As they spoke, she took a second gulp and allowed the night to take her wherever it willed.

———

GARRETT CROSSED THE THRESHOLD, plunging into the jet-black before him. "Jean!" he shouted, hoping she'd answer him this time, any response to give him a direction to strive for. Upon entering this realm of sturdy shadows, he bopped his forehead on a crossbeam, hard enough to cause a bright square to flash before his closed eyes. His skull throbbed, the knock sending a shockwave through the epicenter of his brain. He blinked several times, unable to tell the difference between his inner eyelids and the dark outside. Shaking his head, he plucked his phone from his pocket and threw light at the pitch black. It helped. Not much, but enough to avoid any potential hazards—mainly from stepping on a broken beer bottle left behind by some vagrant drunk or reckless, partying teenagers.

Garrett pushed through the murk, calling his sister's name

every few seconds. She continued to remain mute, leaving him to wander aimlessly through the dark, hoping he'd happen upon her, some answers, the reason she'd left the house and gone wandering out here all alone.

Why are you doing this to me, Jean? he wanted to ask her. A quick image flashed through his mind, him holding his sister against the wall, his hands around her throat, choking the life from her eyes.

He'd quickly scrubbed the thought and chastised himself for thinking of such a thing, even if it was only for a second. Not like he could control his thoughts—sometimes his brain just produced things he didn't wish to see; there was little resistance against these snapshots. It had always been that way. Hell, it was where half his story ideas came from. Quick snippets of some imaginary scenario that scaled into some larger picture, a story, a plot, and characters.

But this...this image of him cornering his sister, choking her until her eyes expanded and, eventually, went cold, dark, and dead, did not sit well with him.

He avoided running into another crossbeam, ducking underneath, and traveling further into the unknown.

Then he heard it. A whisper. Someone whispering to themselves like a prayer, although it sounded like the same words repeated over and over again. He could almost make them out, could almost determine what the hoarse voice was relaying to the all-encompassing dark.

The Sea, the Stars.

Yes, that was it. *The Sea, the Stars* on repeat, like a mantra. The phrase brought cold bumps to his flesh, and he couldn't fight the shiver that danced along the back of his neck, the icy spread across his shoulders.

"Jean..."

It had to be her. Right? It couldn't have been someone else. He'd seen her, saw her drifting toward the mouth of the pier, that unbreakable wall of darkness, and go inside. There couldn't have been anyone else in here, or, at least, there *shouldn't* have been anyone else here. This was not a place to hang out, to linger, to *chant* things about seas and stars. And although no one in their right mind would travel under here at this ungodly hour, Garrett felt the presence of someone else besides himself, besides his sister, an unknown being that felt bigger, taller, and wider than anyone he'd ever met in his entire life. A godlike attendant lurking somewhere just over his shoulder. Garrett shivered, unable to shake the cold from his bones, much too scared to confront this hulking intruder.

He ignored his instinct to run away, a victory of sorts, and then pushed through the dark, wandering farther, weaving between the beams of this secret place. It was impossible not to feel like Alice tumbling down the rabbit hole, watching sensibilities and perceptions reshape themselves, transform into nonsensical lunacies and peculiar illusions.

Feeling woozy from the experience, he rested his hand on a nearby beam to steady himself. There, he paused to catch his breath. He stared at the space between the two rows of vertical beams, an unobstructed glance into the pier's cavernous length.

There, he saw her.

Jean.

His instinct was to run to her. Abandon all caution and just sprint toward her dreamy appearance, ignoring every instinct that told him there was something very wrong taking shape in the dark. And so, he did. He launched himself from his position against the beam, taking off toward his sister, his arms spreading to embrace her the second he reached her.

But he stopped about six feet away, the second his phone's faded blue light illuminated her face, her hands, her entire image.

"Holy sh—Jean?"

Her eyelids fluttered. Behind them, her pupils and irises were gone, erased, and all that remained were two milky white orbs shining against the wall of night. Dark smears like chocolate syrup stained her lips, her chin, her cheeks. She looked like a baby after a first go with pureed prunes. Her hands were also covered in the filth.

Her hands...

He noticed the object she was holding, recognizing it almost immediately. *A conch.* The same fluids that muddied her face dripped from the conch's impossibly dark slit. It looked like a giant bleeding ear. Garrett projected the light a little farther behind his sister. About six feet back, the opened chest lay on the sand. Green light glowed from its base, fading quickly like cooling embers.

Garrett let the light fall on Jean once again. He opened his mouth to speak, but his throat was dry and whatever he was going to say was gone from his thoughts.

Then, Jean's eyes returned. He noticed the fear that held them hostage, like they'd just learned a terrible knowledge, something that could never be forgotten, a secret her ears should not have heard.

"*Garrett,*" she said, her voice trembling, an uneven sound that struck a chord inside him, one that let him know that after tonight...things would never be the same.

Then Jean collapsed on the sand.

SIX

Jean was on the couch, wrapped in several blankets and blowing on the steaming cup of coffee she held with both hands.

Garrett leered at her from the loveseat.

"What?" she asked.

He blinked several times, then looked sideways at her.

"You're staring," she added, irritated.

"You went out in the middle of the night, Jean," he said, his parental tone like a Brillo pad on her eardrums. "You left the house. I was worried sick."

She wanted to say something nasty like, *But were you?* Somehow, she kept the words to herself.

"We just went over this." She took a sip of coffee, hoping he wouldn't notice the exaggerated eye roll she'd shot him.

Oh, he noticed. Look at that face.

Garrett hated the eye roll. If she had insulted his writing, it would have pissed him off less. The eye roll was a trigger, and she had pulled it with glee.

"I want to know why you left. What the hell were you thinking?" He wasn't giving up. Wouldn't let it go until she said something that satisfied him. He was worse than her dating prospects over the last few years, men and women that always wanted to know the answer to everything, every goddamn reason why she did the things she did, said the things she said. It was annoying, the reason she was still single. Well, *one* of them. "I want to know. You owe me an explanation."

"I don't owe you shit, Garrett. I told you—I must have been sleepwalking."

"Sleepwalking all the way to the beach? Under the pier? And with the chest? And Christ, Jean...what was that stuff all over your face? It was like...motor oil or something. You still have a smear near your mouth."

She touched the exact spot where the conch's nectar had dribbled down her chin. "I don't know...I don't remember."

His head fell back, eyes fixating on the ceiling, and he grunted with frustration. "You're killing me."

"Oh, sorry to put you out. I know how precious your sleep is to you."

"Now you're starting to get it." He stood up, brushing off his knees, the sand that clung to his pajama bottoms. "Can I go to bed now? Without you wandering off in the middle of the night to go do...whatever the hell that was back there?"

"You're such a dick."

Another long sigh. "Come on, Jean. I'm trying here."

"That's a first." She sipped her coffee, not caring about the too-hot temperature. A part of her enjoyed the burn, the lingering flare of pain, the potential blister.

"I didn't expect you to be here with me," her brother said. "I wasn't expecting company, and I sure wasn't expecting to have to babysit my little sister this week."

"Sorry to put you out. But that's me. Isn't it? Always

annoying you." She wanted to cry but fought the urge to do so in front of him. He didn't deserve those tears.

"I am doing the best I can. I'm trying to clean out this place, get started on the new novel—which has been a fucking disaster lately, thanks for asking."

She wanted to hurl the closest thing she could find at his head—which, comically, was the unread copy of Garrett's first book. *Unread* because the paperback's spine wasn't cracked and *unread* because she was fairly certain Uncle Jerry had never learned how to read.

"And then *you*," Garrett said accusatorily. "I have to take care of you. Make sure you're taking your medicine, make sure you're safe..."

"If I'm a burden, I'll just go slit both of my wrists right now and be done with it. You'll never have to see or deal with me again. Would that help?" She held out both wrists. "I'll even let you do the honor."

"Jean." His gaze did a complete one-eighty, his caustic mood gone, replaced by sadness and concern, and now he was looking to end this fight. She still wanted to hit him in the face with his own words. There was something magically ironic about that.

"You can tell the police you took no part in it."

"Jean."

"I'll write a nice little suicide letter. It'll be a squeaky-clean case."

"*Jean.*"

"Better yet—maybe you should write it. You're a writer. Bet you'd spin a good suicide note, sick fuck you are." She motioned to the cover of the novel. *Flowers in the Garden of Death* had a lovely depiction of skeletons in a flower bed, pretty flowers blooming up through the skeletons' exposed ribcages and eye sockets.

"That's enough," he said firmly. She knew she'd won, journeyed to the center of him and detonated the bomb within. "Fuck is wrong with you? Why would you joke like that?"

"Who said I was joking?"

He glared at her, harder than he had earlier. "Do I need to call someone now?"

"Do you?"

She wasn't serious. Not now. There was a difference between now and when she'd actually done it. Then, it had felt like there was no hope, no way out, and the only way to escape the perpetual torment was to cut and bleed out. Leave her body the only way she knew how. But here, strangely, she felt safe. She hated to admit that her brother's presence might have something to do with it. Just him *being here* made her feel safe, okay, far from the depression and inescapable dread. At least for the time being.

Even if he was being a complete asshole. He was here.

"I'm okay," she admitted. "Sorry. I was kidding. Please. Go to bed. I'll go to sleep too."

He kept his eyes on her. Studied her, attempting to seek out the truth her eyes might have been hiding. There was no breaking his concentration.

"I'm serious," she said convincingly enough.

"Okay." He surrendered, finally, and warm relief flooded her veins. "Please don't make me regret this."

She nodded. *Everything is okay,* that nod said.

And for the moment, she believed that was true.

AFTER HE WATCHED her fall asleep on the couch, Garrett snuck into the living room and grabbed the treasure chest off the coffee table. He checked to make sure the conch was inside. It was, sitting there in the shadows of the room, no green light pulsating from within. He'd already convinced himself he'd imagined that light under the pier. He'd found no traces of its source. Logic prevailed, and his imagination, coupled with his extreme drowsiness, was the only rational explanation.

As he held the chest close to him, he knew it had to go. He didn't know why, not exactly, and he didn't spend much time trying to figure out why the peculiar thought had entered his head. But he was certain; the object must go far away from this place. *Back into the sea. Where it belongs.* Where it had come from, Garrett thought, judging from the stink of it.

He checked on Jean again, making sure she was asleep. A light, wheezy snore came from her curled body.

Then he headed for the door, the beach, the end of the pier, where he tossed the goddamn chest back into the ocean and prayed he'd never see it again.

THE NEXT MORNING, Garrett awoke to the scent of hot pancakes cooked to perfection. He could almost taste the marsh-mallow-like fluffiness on his tongue when he exited the bedroom and stepped into the hallway. Groggily, he made his way into the kitchen, not bothering to get dressed, still clothed in his PJs.

"What the hell..." he said upon crossing the kitchen's thresh-old, "...is all of this?"

Jean spun toward him, a wild smile flexing across her face. She was all teeth, and he couldn't remember the last time she'd looked this happy. It was jarring, somewhat frightening. On some level he was more terrified of her current mood than what had transpired only a few hours ago under the pier.

"I made pancakes," she said, giddy, bouncing on her heels. It was like she was six again and this was Christmas morning.

"Where..." He looked to the fridge. It was open and there were a few things inside, just some essentials. Milk, eggs. A stick of butter. He turned back and saw the countertop was finely coated with pancake dust, a few globs of batter. "Where did this stuff come from?"

"I went to the store. The one a few blocks down?"

"You...left?"

Her smile disappeared. "Oh shit—Garrett, I'm sorry. I didn't mean to."

He unclenched his jaw. He'd been tough on her last night, *harsh* some might say, and, if he was being honest, he didn't feel good about how he'd treated her. He had been tired, relentlessly exhausted, and Jean's sleepwalking adventure under the boardwalk was just the thing that had pushed him slightly over the edge. "It's okay," he said, not wanting to spark round two.

"Really?"

"Yeah, I was...I was hard on you last night. I'm sorry."

"Gee, thanks, man."

"Let's just hit the reset button. On this whole trip. Start over."

She looked at him, combing him for lies. "You putting me on?"

"No, I'm serious. Let's just forget last night ever happened. Okay?"

"Sure." She bounced on her heels again and then spun back to the pancakes, flipping them before they could burn.

Garrett went to the kitchen table. Stationed in the center of it was the treasure chest, looking much cleaner than it had yesterday. Like someone had given the exterior a good scrub, polished the wooden slats and applied some rust-eater to the hinges and latch. It didn't smell like some pirate's stinky, sweaty love-hole either.

Impossible, he thought. *I threw it in the ocean. I tossed that fucking thing off the pier and watched the waters swallow it up.*

It was true, he had done that in the wee hours of the morning. And unless he'd dreamt it (which was impossible; he knew the difference between dreams and reality), the chest should not have been available for retrieval, even if Jean had discovered what he'd done and gone back out to go fetch it. It was gone. Lost in the depths of the sea. It couldn't have floated; it was too heavy. No possible way it had washed up on the beach.

But clearly something had happened. Clearly someone had found and brought it back to them.

Or Jean did.

He couldn't ignore the look that had been in Jean's eyes when they first pulled it out of the closet. How immediately *obsessed* she'd become with it. How she stared like the chest was some beautiful piece of art, how she surrendered her eyes to its stunning nature.

But there was nothing stunning about it. It was ordinary. Less than ordinary.

It was trash.

"Something wrong?" Jean asked him, grinning.

"No," he lied, forcing a smile of his own. "No, not at all. Hey, I'm going to take this out to the trash," he said. "We agreed to toss it out, so...I'm going to, you know...do that."

The mood in the room suddenly changed. There was a

pause, and in that moment, Jean's face changed. Her smile melted away. There was fire in her eyes, but she immediately extinguished the flames and put that toothy, semi-faux grin back to work. Then, she simply said, "No."

"Huh?"

"You're not throwing it out. We're keeping it."

"But Jean..."

"I said we're keeping it, Garrett. It's ours now."

Garrett opened his mouth to argue, to tell her that the chest belonged in the scrap heap along with Uncle Jerry's other undesirable assets, but there was something in her eyes and voice that kept his words submerged. He could almost hear her whispering her response: *Good boy, Garrett. Keep your mouth shut like a good boy.*

Words his mother used to say.

"Okay," he said, and then had himself a seat at the table.

Jean put a plate of pancakes in front of him. The smell was almost intoxicating, taking him back to those Sunday mornings when they were both kids, when their parents were still together and life was somewhat normal, the only time in his life he could say such a thing. He breathed in those memories, closed his eyes and stole himself away to those past places where things weren't so bad.

Jean ripped him back to reality with a simple sentence: "Oh, and Garrett..."

He opened his eyes, stared at her, and noticed something different about her face. Took all of three seconds to figure it out. It was her eyes. One was a different color than the other. Her left remained hazel, unchanged, but the other...

The right eye held a green shade, electric and alive looking, with a network of whitish strands running through the deep jade surface.

Then she spoke, the words flooding Garrett's veins with a steady, icy flow. "It's best if you don't touch the conch or the chest again. *They* don't like it when you do that."

SEVEN

Later that afternoon, after using the bathroom and while washing her hands, Jean caught a faint whiff of something, an odor she couldn't exactly place. After a quick investigation—sniffing her clothes, her armpits, the surface of the vanity top—she came to the realization that the smell was coming from her own breath. She exhaled into her palm and then sniffed the strangely unpleasant odor, trying to figure out what was causing it. She couldn't; the only thing she'd eaten so far today was the pancakes, and the sweet maple syrup after-scent had faded hours ago.

What the hell is that? she thought, and the second she asked herself that question, she realized the smell had a lingering salty, fishy quality to it.

She immediately reached for her toothbrush and favorite toothpaste, and went to work on her teeth, making sure to brush in the deep pockets of her mouth, where the bad smell was likely coming from. Maybe something she'd eaten yesterday

(*the black egglike jelly*)

got stuck back there and was fouling up her breath.

She brushed well and spit a white foamy stream into the sink and then rinsed her mouth with water. She scanned her reflection in the mirror. She noticed her irises, the different colors, but that wasn't what drew her in, what caused her to keep surveying the image before her, the noticeable changes taking place. The thickness of her body—her muscles specifi-cally—that she seemingly gained overnight gripped her atten-tion. But it wasn't just that. No, what attracted her gaze was the lone mark that had appeared on her neck, just behind her right ear. A red, irritated blemish that reminded her of a nasty mosquito bite but slightly larger. When she leaned in, she saw it was in the shape of a crescent moon.

Weird...

Putting her fingers on the small wound, she winced. The pain was slight but enough to drum up some concern. She didn't remember receiving this injury, but then again, she didn't remember a wink from last night's midnight stroll either. She did remember waking up and then going back to sleep. Only... when she woke up after that, she was under the pier, her brother was there with his mouth hanging agape in the darkness that surrounded them.

Even this morning had been a blur. She remembered cooking the pancakes but couldn't remember where the ingredi-ents had come from. She did recall telling Garrett she'd run to the store, but...

Had she?

She couldn't remember.

Her mind pictured the chest, the conch within. Black spilling out of its slit, the curved ear of the fancy shell.

What is happening to me?
What did I do?

When she looked at herself in the mirror, she was afraid she might eventually answer these questions...and discover so much more.

GARRETT LABORED over the first sentence, but finally the words came, his brain telling his fingertips the correct keys to stroke, and when it was finished, he had it. A first sentence. A start. More than he had had the day before. It felt like he'd finally released a breath he'd been holding in for several minutes. He even sat back in his chair, almost exhausted from the energy spent trying to crank out those fourteen words. Not perfect words. But words were words and he'd take anything at this point.

Just plow through this first draft, he thought, *and fix every-thing later.*

That was how he'd approach this novel, which was contrary to the way he had written the first one. With that one, he'd been meticulous with the first draft, combing over it daily, revising and fixing what he'd written the day prior before moving to the next chapter. By the end, he'd had a pretty solid first draft that had only required some minor editing in subsequent revisions.

But he didn't have the time for that method now. Now, it was burn through this bastard at a frenzied pace, make the corrections later.

Just get it fucking written.

Over the next minutes he put together a sloppy paragraph, and an hour after that he had managed two pages.

He knew the writing was trash, almost every word of it, but two pages felt like an unwinnable victory. Two pages was like finding a well while lost in the middle of the desert. Two pages was progress and progress was welcome even if he loathed the content.

And he did loathe it.

He saved the draft and closed his laptop. Listened to the silence.

No television, no garbage bags being opened and filled with Uncle Jerry's less than desirable items.

Nothing at all.

It was as if the world was holding in a breath, and that put Garrett on edge.

The last thing Jean had said to him echoed through his thoughts: *They don't like it when you do that.*

Just what the hell did that mean? And who were *they* exactly? It was so weird, so unlike Jean—everything from the selected words to the tone she had used—that he just let it go. Pretended like she hadn't spoken at all. The warning (if he could call it that) had never happened as far as he was concerned.

But it had happened, and the more he thought about it, the more it bothered him. He wanted to ask her to explain herself, but right now wasn't the best time.

Right now, he needed to clear his mind and write.

EMERGING from the bedroom doubling as his office, Garrett traveled the length of the hallway, yawning and stretching his limbs. He made for the kitchen, the Keurig he'd brought from his New York City apartment—the one machine he couldn't live without besides his cell phone and laptop. He poured himself some pumpkin spice and then sat at the table across from Jean. She was doodling on a sketch pad. "What'cha doodling there?"

She ignored him. Didn't look up. Kept sketching, the tip of her pencil moving back and forth on the surface, the pace rushed, that constant rustling sound of graphite meeting paper. Jean's hair dangled in front of her face, wet and stringy. He couldn't see her eyes.

"Sis?"

She stopped but didn't look up. Then she was at it again, working the pencil harder than before, as if she were against the clock and needed to finish before some great cataclysmic event transpired.

"Jean?" He leaned in, trying to catch a glimpse at what she was doing. She covered up the drawing with both arms and pulled the sheet closer to her chest. She hesitated, and Garrett heard a low sound come from within her, one that almost sounded like an animal defending its territory, guttural and feral. "Are you okay?" he asked, and at this point, any answer would level his increasing anxiety.

He half expected her to start barking at him, but she didn't. She chose to ignore him instead.

"Jean, what's gotten into you lately?" He tapped his knuckles on the table, hoping to break her from this vow of silence. "Hello? Are you going to talk to me? Are you pissed at me? At least tell me what I did."

She glanced up. He could see her eyes now, and what stared back frightened him. A cold web shot across his shoulders. Her eyes were glassy and bloodshot, like she'd taken some punches and all the capillaries had broken at once. Her skin was pallid, the color of soft moonlight.

"*Shut. Up,*" she growled, and then went back to her drawing, which Garrett could see was a sketch above her talents, unless she'd taken up some art class in the last few years. Ever since they were kids, Jean had wanted to draw and paint and craft, be artistic any way she could. But the sad fact was, she had not a single artistic bone in her body. He'd encouraged her throughout their youth, of course—he wasn't cruel. But the truth? Her sketches and paintings were messy, hectic, and just… well, plain *bad*. Art was subjective, that was true—a fact Garrett knew very, very well and believed in wholeheartedly—but Jean's "art" was something a harsh critic might have been quick to laugh at.

But the sketch he'd caught a quick peek of…it looked good. He couldn't make out exactly what it was, but the depiction had a definitive shape and the shading looked professional. Like the panel of a comic book artist's layered sketch. For all he knew the illustration could have been no better than the terrible ones she'd made throughout high school, but he didn't think so. This…this was something else.

"Jean, just show me what you're—"

She pounded her fist on the table. The pink eraser jumped. The dark surface of his coffee rippled angrily. "I said, *shut up.*"

"Jean, why are you acting this way?"

She leered at him with those awful eyes.

"And what is up with your eyes? Do you need a doctor? Can you…Christ, can you even see out of them?"

At this she smiled. "I can see just fine, Garrett. Better than I ever have."

This couldn't be true, but he sensed no lie.

"Jean, you're starting to..." *Frighten me* was what he wanted to say, but he couldn't admit that, could he? He was the big brother here, a protector of sorts. *Protectors are not afraid. They can't afford to be.* "You're starting to concern me," was the statement he decided on. "I think we should head back to the city tomorrow. We can drop by the hospital and have them—"

"I'm not going anywhere, Garrett. I'm staying here. Where I belong."

She went back to the drawing and didn't speak another word.

Garrett watched her, unable to respond. Her attitude was not like the girl he'd known his whole life. Not when they were kids, not in the past few days.

What did she mean, *Where I belong? Here? At Uncle Jerry's place?*

None of it made sense.

So, Garrett did the only thing he could think of, the only thing that made sense.

He ignored it. For he had a novel to write.

LATER THAT NIGHT, after he was pretty sure his sister had gone to sleep, Garrett sat behind the computer desk and tapped away on some fresh words. He'd found a pretty good stride, hammering out two thousand words in a little over two hours. *Killing Spaces* had reached a respectable five thousand words, and once he had crossed that threshold, it felt like he'd climbed to a monumental height of an advanced mountain trail. There was still plenty of mountain left to travel, but the relief that he'd gotten this far washed over him like a brisk wave. He felt alive again, and for the first time since he'd penned that freshman publication, it felt like he had known what he was doing all along.

Maybe I am good at this, he thought to himself, leaning back in the chair, and cracking his knuckles, admiring the not-so-perfect words before him.

A thud on the window behind him jolted his entire body. At first he thought he'd been punched by something in the back of the head; the sound was that loud and reverberated down his spine, sinking into his toes. He spun around, facing the direction of the disruptive noise. He found himself staring out the window, into the blackened night. On the glass, a smear ran down both sashes. A slimy splat, thick and translucent, a gummy explosion.

Garrett extricated himself from the chair and leaned closer. He was hesitant to get too close in case there was another assault. The offender might decide to throw a rock next, and Garrett wasn't too keen on taking a beach stone to the face, along with the shards of glass that would follow in its wake. Instinctively, he searched the room for the first weapon he could find, which happened to be the newish hammer they had used on the treasure chest back on day one. Arming himself with the cheap hand tool, gripping the cherry-red handle, he eyed the glass, the night outside, expecting some specter to show itself, a ghastly white face to intrude on the darkened exterior.

But he kept his distance, backing away from the window and heading toward the door, the hallway. He went to the kitchen and grabbed a flashlight, hurried out the front door and stepped foot onto the front porch. On his way, he noticed Jean was missing from the couch and hoped to God she was in the second bedroom, asleep and dreaming happy dreams. He was too curious to see what was waiting for him outside to go back and check on her. He felt safe with his flashlight and hammer.

Probably just a kid, playing a joke. Or a seagull taking a shit on the window.

He wasn't sure he believed either of those scenarios, but it was better than the other thoughts kicking around his weary mind, that the vandal was perhaps looking to break in. To rob the place, to murder them.

This wasn't the safest of neighborhoods. And it *was* off-season; he remembered Uncle Jerry telling them once that robberies and break-ins were five times more likely to occur during the fall and winter months.

He had his hammer. He felt safe enough.

What if they have a gun?

He didn't dwell on that notion, couldn't. He marched around the side of the house, rounded the back left corner, and entered the backyard. Scanning the dunes behind the property, he only saw sand and grass and the shroud of night that surrounded everything, filled the world like some viscous fluid poured over.

Turning his attention to the window, the smell hit him all at once. An overpowering fishy stench that turned his head, made him cough and cover his mouth and nose with the crook of his arm. After thirty seconds or so, the smell faded some but not nearly enough. He approached the object on the ground in front of the window, and the closer he got, the stronger it became.

"Oh fuck," he muttered, feeling his gorge rise. He hunched over, certain he'd lose his dinner over this. As he gagged, he saw what had been thrown against the window. A butchered fish carcass lay on a short patch of marram grass, the guts all spilled out and haphazardly spread across the neighboring concrete walkway.

Garrett controlled his stomach and the need to expel his dinner. He continued to cover his nose as he crept closer, getting a better glimpse at the dead fish. Its shiny, metallic-looking skin reflected a considerable amount of moonlight. A single eye beamed at him, lifeless and cold and penetrating.

Garrett shuddered, then looked over his shoulder expecting to see the offender watching from the near distance, getting a good laugh at Garrett's disgust. Tightly gripping the hammer, he saw nothing but black sky. The dunes. The wind running through the tufts of grass, gently pushing their leafy strands this way and that. The houses down the block with their lights off, their owners either gone for the impending winter or sleeping snugly inside.

No guilty party observing the scene, reveling in Garrett's misery.

Garrett found a garbage bag pinned under some rocks near the edge of the patio. He'd brought out the bags earlier to clean up the backyard, throw away a few things, and must have forgotten he'd left this one behind. He put his hand in the bag and used it as a glove to pick up the fish guts, and then pulled his arm through, allowing the guts to remain inside while avoiding direct contact with his skin. Then he disposed of the nastiness in the garbage can on the side of the house, immediately lugging the whole thing to the curb, hoping everything they'd culled from the house so far would get picked up soon. The collective funk of their uncle's trash was starting to become a permanent fixture on the block. He wondered if the neighbors would complain.

Next, he went back into the house and took a shower,

washing off the fish-gut stink that seemed to infiltrate his every pore. Then he forced himself to bed and tried his hardest to fall asleep.

But the stench of dead fish followed him there, and the faint whispers of a thousand ghostly voices kept him awake.

EIGHT

He hadn't noticed it last night, but one of Uncle Jerry's gutters had fallen off on one side (closest to their neighbor) and was hanging low. One of the nails must have popped out, so Garrett took the ladder from the garage and his trusty hammer, climbed up and started to reattach the gutter to the siding. It was a quick job, and when he was finished, he climbed back down, hammer in hand, and turned around to find himself staring into an expression built by concern.

"Hi," Patti said, her nervous fingers working the muscles of her opposite hand. "I was wondering if I could have a word."

Garrett immediately thought back to the other day. Jean pouting her lips and, in that lovesick voice, saying, *"Oh, Garrett, you big writer man you!"*

He swallowed, shook his head, and immediately cleared the spicy thought from his mind. "Morning, Patti. What can I do for you?"

She looked pale. "I...well, I have something I'd like to talk to you about."

"Have anything to do with the stinky fish you left on the porch the other night?"

She reacted like Garrett had unceremoniously told her to go fuck herself. "What in tarnation are you talking about?"

In response, he flared an eyebrow.

She stared dumbly. "I don't...we didn't leave any fish on your porch. We would have, but you sounded like you weren't too keen on the idea. We respect boundaries here."

He wasn't buying it. Not at first. But the longer he studied her, the more he sensed she was telling the truth.

"Did you see anyone sneaking around the backyard last night? Around three, four o'clock?"

Patti ruffled her brow. "That's what I've come to talk about."

A pang of surprise spiked through him. "You saw someone? Last night?"

"I've seen someone around here the last few nights, taking a nightly stroll through our yard. Looking in through our window." Patti's face paled some more. "Watching us sleep."

"Jesus Christ," Garrett muttered. The phantom fish smell returned, turning his stomach. Acid ascended his throat, burning the back of his tongue. "Did you recognize the person?"

A slight nod. "It was your sister."

JEAN SOAKED in the bubble bath, running the soapy water over her arms, her neck. Then she tilted her head back against the ceramic tile, stared up at the teal walls of the bathroom. Uncle Jerry hadn't painted the place since they were kids, and the same water-stained tea spots she remembered from her youth still clung to the corners of the shower, only much darker now. The walls needed to be replaced, torn down and treated for mold. She ignored the work that needed to be done in here and concentrated on her own skin. Eventually, her eyes wandered the length of her right arm, settling on her wrist. She'd undone the bandages to air out the incision, let it breathe per the doc's orders. Gently, she washed the wound with a damp rag.

Every time she cleaned it, she couldn't help but wander back to the dark day that had caused this whole mess. Luckily, she was in a good enough headspace to not want to revisit that pain again. The desire to tear open the stitched flesh was gone. That monster inside her that feasted on her positivity and gave birth to negative thoughts had gone into hibernation, to its reclusive cave. It was only a matter of time before it woke up again; she knew that. But next time, when the monster came, she'd be a little more prepared.

And properly medicated, she thought. Hoped.

The pills the doctor at the hospital had given her were helping so far. She hadn't had one intrusive thought since arriving at the shore house. Not a single, split-second image of her harming herself with a razorblade, tying a noose and hanging herself from a tree, or jumping off the Brooklyn bridge. These thoughts that had occurred quite frequently leading up to the day she couldn't bear it anymore.

Before the voices became too much.

She closed her eyes and enjoyed the silence. That moment of nothingness was so serene her body almost didn't know how to process it.

Then she opened her eyes and returned to the stitched line that ran from the base of her palm to one-third of the way down her arm, a six-inch gash so deep it had felt like nothing when the flesh had separated.

She noticed something she hadn't before. The skin near the stitches was discolored, not her usual pale complexion. She brought her wrist before her eyes and ran her fingers over the bumpy, fused skin. The surface was darker, almost gray. When the light above hit the skin just right, it shone with a small brightness, like reflective glass.

What is that? she wondered, studying herself. As she did, the silence was interrupted. Low and sounding as if they were several rooms away, the whispers began. She felt the mood of the room change, an intrusion on this serene moment. Something dark was with her now, but she couldn't see it.

The heel of her foot slipped, slid into the drain stopper, knocking it aside. The pipe began to swallow the bath, gurgling the rush of water. The frothy bubbles shrunk, exposing more of her body, and that was when she noticed the skin around her secret wound wasn't the only thing affected by what was happening here—her legs also wore the mark. A patchwork of silver crust ran down her thighs, covering spots across her knees and ankles, sporadic and distanced every six inches or so. As the drain consumed the last of the water, as she sat in a shallow bath of marshmallowy suds, she ran her fingers over the new skin. The discolored flesh was tough to the touch, and when she tucked her knees close to her chin, she suddenly saw exactly what had grown on the surface of her lower half—scales.

Fish scales, she thought.

And then she started crying as the whispers in the hallway grew closer.

PATTI DROPPED a fresh cup of coffee in front of him. "All writers drink lots of coffee or is that just a stereotype?"

"This writer can't exist without it," he told her, taking that initial sip, not caring how hot it was. Setting the mug on the table, he rested his back against the chair. "So...Jean. You saw her last night?"

Looking away, Patti nodded. "Yes. And the night before. She's quite the night owl." She stationed herself across from him and eyed her own coffee mug. "I'M HOOKED!" was written above a cartoon fisherman in a rowboat, a fish dangling from the end of his line. Below the funny drawing, it read, "ON FISHING."

Garrett refrained from rolling his eyes.

"Are you aware?" she asked.

He blinked, looking away from the mug. "What's that?"

"Aware that she keeps such strange hours?"

He sensed a lie would not help him here. "Yeah, I caught her leaving the other night."

"I don't normally like to pry into other people's business, and I certainly don't like telling folks how to live their lives, but..." She frowned, showing the smallest morsel of empathy. "This is a nice community, sure, but sometimes..." Her face collected in wrinkles then, like her thoughts were fighting for a way past her lips. "What I'm trying to say is—going on a midnight stroll ain't exactly the best idea around these parts, not this time of year. Catch my drift?"

"I catch it. And I'm sorry. We had a talk about it. Won't happen again." He wondered if he sounded as full of shit as he thought he did.

"She's a wanderer. Wanderers are gonna wander." She

flashed a smile that was obviously forced. "She reminds me of your uncle."

"How so?"

Her eyes slimmed. "He used to keep strange hours too. Went fishing late at night or early in the morning depending on your perspective. Tried to get my husband to go with him, tried convincing him those post-midnight hours were the best for catching the 'big ones,' he used to say." She waved a limp wrist. *Pish-posh.* "Pure hogwash, though. My Peter, he's been a fisherman his whole life—his daddy before him and his before him —and he knows the ocean like the back of his hand. 'Night fishing ain't no better,' he'd tell me. So whatever Jerry was after on those midnight fishing trips, surely wasn't no fish."

"Interesting."

"What bothers me about your sister the most is...is what happened last night."

Garrett shifted in his seat like the seat was studded with thorns. "What happened last night?"

"Caught her staring through our window while we were sleeping."

"For real?"

"For real," she repeated, and he could detect no fabrication in her claim. And he would have too—it was a skill he had, one he'd picked up and perfected while writing articles for the Brooklyn Times fresh out of college. Patti held the eyes of someone relaying a true account. "It was...well, the best way to put it—*freaky*."

"I bet. I'm so sorry, Patti. I'll have a talk with Jean and get it all sorted out."

"I don't even think she was aware she was doing it."

Garrett's mouth ran dry. "Sorry?"

"She was just standing there, staring at us, but not *at* us. Her eyes...they were just so...vacant. You know what I mean?"

His tongue probed his inner cheek. He worried she'd see through the dumb face he was fronting. "I'm afraid I don't."

"I guess *sleepwalking* is the proper term for it. Like she was dreaming but awake. Her mouth was moving, and she was whispering things."

Whispering.

"What was she saying?" Garrett asked, feeling a lump coagulate in his throat.

"Heck if I know." The woman shrugged, sipped her coffee. "Couldn't make out a word of it. Gibberish mostly. We tried talking to her through the window, even invited her in. It was cold last night, and she was shivering something fierce. I went to fetch her a blanket and even put on a cup of coffee—but by the time we went outside to go get the poor girl, she was gone."

"Where'd she go?"

Patti gave him a hard stare, like she expected him to know the answer. "I'm assuming she went back to your uncle's place. You didn't hear her come and go last night?"

"I was up late. When did his happen?"

"Three-twenty, thereabouts."

"Nonsense." He jerked his thumb toward the kitchen window. "I would have heard her. I was up. That's around the same time someone chucked a dead fish at my window."

"I'm sorry to say, that's when it occurred."

He shook his head. "Okay, maybe I have my time screwed up. Maybe it was earlier then."

"Maybe. Look, I hope Jean doesn't mind me tattling on her. It's only for her safety, you know."

Garrett waved her off. "No, I'm glad you told me. Jean... she's been having a rough go of things lately."

"Oh?"

He debated whether to spill the family beans. In the end he decided it couldn't hurt. Patti seemed harmless, and, honestly, she was the only person he could talk to, get advice from out here, this far from home. "She hurt herself back in New York."

"Hurt herself..." Patti's confusion melted away, and the realization took over. "The bandage on her wrist..."

"Yeah." Garrett sighed. He felt a little ashamed for telling Patti this. Like it was Jean's story to tell, not his. "Our family has a history of depression."

"I'm so sorry."

"Thanks. It's been difficult. Thought bringing her here would do her some good," he lied, "thought it might, I don't know—shake her out of it? That the change in environment might help some. But...I don't know. Depression isn't something you can really run away from, is it?"

Patti wrinkled her nose. "I'm certainly no expert, but my guess is—no. Depression ain't something so easily defeated. She'll need more than a vacation to slay that dragon."

"Yeah, you're probably right." He tapped the table with his fingers. "Went through something similar with our mother. She had similar episodes, but they were complicated by her excessive drug and alcohol use."

"Hmm. I've known a few of those in my time."

"So, right, our family kind of sucks."

"But hey—you turned out all right."

He wanted to laugh at that. "Guess I'm kind of the black sheep, you could say. Jean might tell you differently. She loves to psychoanalyze me, tell me how messed up I am."

"I bet. You and your sister seem pretty close." Patti's eyes sparkled as if she had some foreknowledge of their relationship, that her *bet* was intentionally wrong. Like she was testing Garrett to spill more of their dynamic.

"We haven't been for a long, long time," he admitted.

"But now?"

"We're getting there. Mending old wounds, I guess you could say."

"Well, that's a happy story."

"Did Uncle Jerry talk about us much?"

Her eyes swept the room. "What do you mean?"

"When we met you the other day, you made it seem like he talked about us. Which is weird, considering we haven't seen or spoken to him since our mother's funeral. Hardly knew the guy, really."

"He spoke of you two. Not often."

"Hmm." That he spoke of them at all was quite surprising. "What did he say?"

"Oh, this and that. Very seldomly. Like I said the other day, he was quite proud of your book, you being an author. Quite proud."

"I'm shocked."

"Why's that?"

Garrett rubbed his hands together. "I guess...I don't know, the guy never called me, never even wrote an email. Never knew he cared about us at all, let alone some novel I wrote."

"Well...people are different. They express themselves in different—and sometimes—unusual ways. If I know one thing, it's that your uncle loved you and your sister. Very much."

He sniffled, a touch of sadness needling the back of his eye sockets. "Thank you for that, Patti."

"My pleasure." She flashed him a warm smile. He was about to thank her for the coffee and make for the exit when she said, "Your mother...your uncle did speak of her some."

"Oh?"

"Said you left home when things got bad. Is that right?"

His sadness turned to something else, something he hadn't felt in a long, long time. "Yeah, that's right. I went off to school. College."

"Ah. He said you felt guilty for leaving."

Garrett glared ahead, not breaking eye contact with the woman. He wasn't sure why she was bringing this up, didn't understand the point. "I don't know what this has to do with—"

"I see a deep pain in you, Garrett Pryce. Now, you might be able to fool other people, your sister mostly, but you can't get anything past ol' Patti here. Understand?"

He almost pushed himself away from the table and left, but something kept him seated. Maybe it was the woman herself, how he'd like to learn more about her, maybe use her quirks and *off*-ness to help build a character in a future work. He often subjected himself to uncomfortable social situations for the sake of absorbing some great tidbits to use in his writing.

"Sure," he simply said, then returned the cup of coffee to his lips.

"So, do you? Feel guilty?" Patti's bluntness altered his mood. "It's okay to talk about things, Garrett. Might do you some good to let it out." Her words seemed genuine, and Garrett didn't detect any hostility.

"I guess. I wish I'd been there, sure."

"Do you think Jean would have turned out differently if you had stayed?" She lowered her eyes, concentrating on the hand-drawn strawberry vines that decorated the placemat before her.

"I don't know. Maybe." He bit his lip. "Probably. Yes."

"My husband," she started, and the way she spoke, Garrett knew he was in for a story, a long one. "He worked on commercial fishing boats his entire life, all the way up until the day he retired—only but a few years ago—and he loved every single moment of it. Gosh, even the bad times."

"That's great, Patti," he said, checking his watch. Time was creeping into the afternoon, and he had writing to do. "And I don't mean to sound rude, but does this have anything to do with Jean and last night?"

She stared him straight on, leery-eyed. "I'm getting there, boy."

He clammed up, sat back, and listened.

"One day, just a month before Peter's retirement, something happened on the boat. Miles out, a faulty thru-hull caused the liner to sink...and sink pretty damn fast." She scoffed. "Rumor had it that someone had tampered with the boat, that the damage couldn't have been caused by any other means, but that was never proven. In any case, everyone was instructed to abandon ship—there was nothing they could do to repair the damage and make it safely back to the dock. All but one man listened to the captain—a man named Morris Courtney. He was this tough old-timer, had this big ego and a ain't-gonna-best-me mentality. He wasn't going to leave that boat no matter what. No, sir. He was hellbent on doing anything he could to stop the ol' gal from sinking, despite the captain's command. Morris was gonna fix it or die trying."

She paused to catch her breath.

"What happened then?" Garrett asked.

"What happened then was the son of a bitch drowned while everyone else got away. Slipped beneath the surface along with some of the wreckage and never came back up. His body washed up on shore a couple of weeks later."

"That's awful." Garrett still wondered what the moral of this story was and why he was supposed to give a shit about it. "No one else died?"

"Nope. The abandoners...they survived. And my point is, Garrett—sometimes, in order to survive, you have to know when you've lost. Know when to abandon. Ships." Her eyes drilled into his with a coldness that wasn't there before. "People."

"You're saying...I was right to leave them? My mother, my sister."

Patti shrugged. "I'm saying you did your best, but don't chastise yourself for wanting to survive. To better yourself. Shed yourself of all that guilt. I can see it clinging to you, weighing you down like an anchor."

Garrett looked to the far corner of the room, his eyes settling on a pirate's galleon enclosed in a glass bottle.

"I think about it a lot," he said, fixating on Patti's story, the ship, wondering if he would have been the first to jump. "I think if I hadn't left them, that if I'd done more, then we'd all still be together. And that everything would be okay. That Mom would be alive, and Jean would be...would be better."

"Maybe she'd be worse." Her tone was gentle and meant to soothe him, but the message was anything but comforting. "I know it's tough to let go of the choices we make, but the past is in the past and we can't change that. You can only affect the future."

Garrett nodded. "Wise words, Patti. You're like my own personal fortune cookie."

The compliment made her smirk. "You're a riot. You sure you don't write funny books?"

"I better get going," he said, rising to his feet.

"Your uncle was on that boat," she said, stopping him immediately.

"Sorry?"

"Your uncle, Jerry," she said, that sly, knowing smirk still resting beneath her nose. "Peter told me he was the first to jump."

NINE

When Jean opened her eyes, she saw a hand gliding before her. Back and forth. Sort of floating there. Took a second for her eyes to adjust and locate the waver's wrist, the rest of the arm. Then the fingers snapped, rapidly and repeatedly, spearing her attention. A few more waves. Behind the hand, the television glowed with interference, the staticky crunch of no reception droning on. The black and white fuzz had this hypnotic quality to it, and its lure was too captivating to look anywhere else. If she stared at it for a few more seconds, she'd undoubtedly get lost there for a long, long time.

"Jean?" a voice said, sounding like it had come from a dream she had just awoken from. Deep. Echoing.

Was she dreaming still? Was this real life?

She couldn't remember anything after the bath, but even those ten minutes alone were hazy, not fully there for her memory to grasp.

What's happening to me?

She glanced up at her brother. Then the window, that square of black showing off the night's boldest quality. Back to

Garrett. She didn't know why but she felt guilty for something.

"What are you doing?" he asked.

The television continued to project its static noise. She was drawn to it; the moving pixels begged for her eyes.

"I don't know," she admitted. "What am I doing?"

Garrett bent to one knee. "Jean...I think you really need to see someone. Like...tonight. I mean...Jesus. Look at yourself."

He held his phone in front of her, the camera facing her so she could see herself. The second she laid eyes on the image, she wondered what was wrong with the lens, why it was displaying her like that. Or what grotesque filter Garrett had applied just to mess with her. The concerned lines etched into his forehead told her he wasn't putting her on, that the reflected image before her wasn't some distortion. It was real.

She really looked that bad.

"What..." she said, feeling breathless.

"Come on. Let me help you to the car."

Garrett put an arm around her, but she pushed him away.

"No," she said, staring at her face. The skin around the eye that had changed color was sagging and bruised. She lowered the camera to have a look at her neck, behind her ear where the crescent moon had appeared on her flesh. It was still there, angrier now, swollen and radish red. Puffy and possibly infected. She noticed another mark on the opposite side, not as prominent as its predecessor. A smeary pink contusion that would eventually blossom into something definable rested an inch below her ear lobe.

Besides the new additions to her facial features, she couldn't help but notice her head itself had changed. The shape of it. She couldn't explain what it was—whether it was smaller or wider, larger or had malformed like the rind of some rotting fruit —but she knew it was *off*. Given the stare Garrett was beaming her way, he saw it too.

"Jean, I insist," he said, and the timbre of his voice elevated her sense of panic.

"Okay," she resigned. "Let's go."

"Fucking finally," he said, putting her arm around his neck and lifting her off the floor.

HE WAS glad Jean had cooperated. He didn't want to have to drug her, though he couldn't imagine himself doing that. In any case, getting her to the car was no easy feat. Despite her weighing about a buck-twenty (sopping wet), he struggled with getting her to the front door and down the steps. It was like her body was filled with cured concrete.

Garrett managed the best he could, lugging her over to the passenger's seat. He opened the door, assisted her inside. Buckled her in like a good big brother. Her glazed eyes ran over him, and a languid smile stretched across her face. Her teeth were outlined in black, like they were suddenly rotting at the gumline.

"Such a good big brother, Garrett," she said dreamily, her eyelids fluttering.

"Yeah," he said. "That's me."

Then he got in the car, cranked the engine, and pulled out of the driveway.

As he drove past Patti's house, he noticed the lights were on. He half-expected her to be on her front porch, watching them drive off. Staring. Snooping. Trying to obtain the juicy gossip to spread around the neighborhood, though, how many neighbors were left on the block he didn't know, but it couldn't have been a large number. He figured she was just a lonely old woman whose husband was hardly home, a man who spent most of his retirement fishing with the boys, and she just needed someone to talk to. No harm in that, he supposed. No harm at all.

He gunned the car down the block, made the necessary turns that Google Maps shouted at him. Blowing through the empty streets, he couldn't ignore how alone he felt out here. Not a single soul traveled the sidewalks. No other cars occupied the road. It was just after sundown and the streets should have been showing some evidence that life existed out here, but the town was as dead as Jean currently looked.

He took the directions to the town's outskirts. He saw the bridge that connected Tripp's Isle to the mainland peeking just over the horizon. Ignoring the speed limit, he accelerated toward their destination. His foot felt like a brick on the gas pedal.

The bridge finally appeared before them and Garrett hit the gas even harder once it was in view, easing the pedal to the floor. The car sped over the bridge. While they passed under the dim orange bridge lights, Garrett stole a glimpse at his sister. Her eyes were closed, and her chest was expanding and contracting. She was alive, but he had no clue what was wrong with her. The bruises and marks on her flesh were symptoms of something, but he couldn't venture a guess, not even with his wild imagination. Dr. Google had been less than helpful in the diagnosis department.

Whatever she had, Garrett assumed there was no name for it yet.

Once over the bridge, Garrett leveled off the speed, fearing a cop would be tucked behind a cluster of trees up ahead. It was the perfect speed trap, but they had no time to waste. He eased off the pedal and brought the car under fifty, obeying the forty-five mile-per-hour speed limit, and continued down the road flanked by towering bushy oaks and full pines. The road seemed much longer now than it had coming in, and Garrett figured that was the way with roads; always longer when you have someplace to be.

After ten minutes, he began to worry. It shouldn't have taken this long to reach the main highway. Glancing at the app, it still showed he had another ten minutes to go, the same amount it had been when he hit the bridge ten minutes *ago*. Time wasn't adding up. Sweat beaded on his brow. His heart rate accelerated like a car engine with a madman behind the wheel; he could feel the beat throbbing in his temples.

"What the hell?" he asked himself, and when he came to the bridge again, he felt as if the bottom of the world had dropped out from beneath him.

"Jean," he said, parking in front of the bridge's entrance. "Jean, wake up."

She didn't move.

"Fuck. JEAN!" He leaned over and shook her, but she showed no signs of life. He shook her again with more urgency this time. "Jean, please wake up."

Finally, she stirred. "Wha..." she managed groggily. "What's happening?"

"There's something wrong," Garrett said, and he hated the way his voice sounded. Like a kid telling his parents the boogeyman had invaded his closet, being more afraid to admit such a thing than the thing itself.

"What?" she asked. The moonlight really brought out the

bruises on her face, accentuating them in such a violent way, making her look way worse than she had back at the house.

He chose to ignore her condition for now. What difference did her symptoms make if they couldn't reach the people who could treat them?

His airway felt like a knotted tube. "We crossed the bridge, but somehow we ended up back here."

"How?"

"I don't know. The fucking GPS isn't working, either." He tapped the screen. A vertical green line appeared in the center of the map, and the screen glitched, pixelating for about three seconds before returning to the map's dark-view mode again. The green line blipped out, came back, and then disappeared once again.

"I don't understand," she said, almost slurring the words.

He almost explained the situation again, then realized he'd be wasting his breath, his time. "Forget it. Go back to sleep."

He hit the gas and sped over the bridge. Drove for ten minutes before coming to the bottom of the same bridge again. This time he kept his eyes on the map, watching his progress. But it seemed like there was no progress, just the stretch of road and the bridge.

"What the fuck..." This couldn't be happening.

But it is, he thought. *It's happening, I can see it happening.*

He tried one more time, taking the bridge and driving past it, keeping his eyes glued to the digital road resting on the dashboard. He even zoomed out some so he could see what was waiting for him up ahead—he wasn't surprised to see a long line that eventually led to the bridge again.

"Fuck!" he said, then pulled over to the side of the road. He got out, phone in hand. He closed Google Maps and did the only thing he could think of at this point—he hit 9-1-1 on the keypad and placed the call.

Static greeted his ear. The call wouldn't go through, and when he looked at the phone, all he saw were pixelated squares dancing on top of each other while the consistent drone of static noise filled in the silence of the surrounding woods.

He wanted to trash the phone on the blacktop, crush the bastard beneath his foot, a sort of payment for the technology's bitter betrayal.

But he refrained from severing his only possible connection to the outside world, even if it was currently nonoperational.

He returned to the car. Jean was leaning back in her seat, snoring.

The road ahead was dark, offering zero hope. Just darkness and darkness beyond that darkness, all light hidden away like any good secret.

He climbed into the driver's seat and drove in the only direction he knew Tripp's Isle would allow him to go—*home*, if he could even call the place such a thing.

TEN

The next morning, Garrett awoke with the world's worst hangover despite not taking a single sip of alcohol the night before. It was like the strange experience on the highway had intoxicated him, left him dehydrated and lacking vital nutrition. Like it had stolen something from him.

He made his way to the bathroom and dry heaved. There was nothing to expunge; not even bile would introduce itself.

Jean was fine, though. She was bouncing around the kitchen, dumping pancake after pancake onto the platter that rested in the center of the kitchen's island. She did so with a proud chef's smile. A heap of scrambled eggs was already plated in the center of the table.

Garrett limped into the room and immediately noticed that Jean's face had gone back to the way it was before, prior to their arrival on Tripp's Isle. Healthy. Free from blemishes of any kind.

"Jean?" he asked, fighting off the spins.

"Brother," she said happily. "You ready for breakfast?"

He was hungry but didn't feel like eating. "I'll pass."

"Come on. I've made enough for the two of us."

He eyed her, and his cautious stare must have tipped her off.

"Something wrong?" she asked, holding out the spatula as if preparing to swat some flies. "Did I do something wrong?"

"No," he said immediately, without thinking. "No, I just don't feel too hot."

"Well, lie down then. Relax. Do you want me to make coffee? I know you can't get your day started without it."

Even the thought of coffee turned his stomach. "I'm fine."

"What about scrambled eggs?" she asked, not taking the hint. "Would you like mustard on them?"

"Mustard?"

"Oh, yes. You must try them with mustard."

Garrett, who thought ketchup on eggs qualified as a mortal sin, scoffed. "You don't put mustard on eggs, Jean. Just...*ew*."

"Have you ever had it?" Her face changed then, lips puckering, like his comment tasted like strong lemons.

"Well...no."

"Then how do you know?" Her eyebrows rose as she waited for his response. "How do you know you don't like something until you've experienced it?"

He sighed. "Because it sounds fucking disgusting."

An unsettling smirk forced its way onto her face. "There's a blurry line between disgusting and divine."

"Well, I disagree." He nodded at her, planning to make a swift exit from this conversation. It was the look in her eyes that made him want to be anywhere else. The dual looks mostly, how the color in one eye seemed to be always changing, a chromatic feature he couldn't help but think was completely unnatural. "I'm going to start on the attic. Have a look around and begin bagging up the trash. When you're done here...wanna help?"

Jean stuck her index finger in the pancake batter, then popped the finger in her mouth. Sucked her finger clean, reveling in the taste of the uncooked concoction. "Sure," she said, after swallowing the batter in one gulp. "I'd love to."

THE ATTIC SMELLED stale and salty but, thank God, it was free from the fishy scent that seemed to permeate almost everything here. Garrett climbed the stairs with the garbage bag in his right hand. A quick scan of the area told him he'd be up here for a while. There were more piles of insignificant collectibles and antiques, and he knew instantly most of the remaining week would be spent up here, going through these items and ultimately throwing away most of them. Whether they held any value or not, Garrett didn't care. He was finished with this place. If he could sell the house as is, he would, but his real estate buddy had told him he'd have to take a decent chunk off the listing price. He wasn't going to sell for ten, fifteen grand less when he could just do the work himself.

But the task was getting to be too much, and with Jean and her peculiar episodes, coupled with trying to keep her safe, adding on the strange occurrences that were taking place at night—well, he was beginning to second guess the decision to haul out every single one of Uncle Jerry's belongings. *Because,* he thought, *let's face it: my sister isn't exactly helping.*

It was a delicate situation. He didn't want to be too hard on her like he had been in the past. He knew she was struggling.

Knew she was dealing with things in her own way, even if it wasn't the best, healthiest approach. She was still trying.

He made his way onto the plywood landing and crawled toward a stack of totes. The attic was too short, so he couldn't stand up. He could crouch and get around the space, but on his knees proved to be the easier method. When he reached the first tote, he lifted the lid and peeked inside. A moldy odor crawled up his nostrils. Smelled like an old, wet newspaper. Pungent but manageable. He dropped the lid on the plywood floor and dug through the tote's contents. The tote contained a wide variety of trash; baseball trophies Uncle Jerry must have earned as a child (weird, considering he'd hardly been the athletic type), Christmas ornaments (Garrett was pretty sure his uncle had been a practicing atheist), and a collection of photo albums (surprising, considering the guy hadn't been too sentimental when it came to family stuff). Garrett went through the albums, flipping through the pages. They went back a few decades. He found pictures of him and Jean, no older than five or six, the two of them playing in the plastic whale pool Uncle Jerry had bought for them at Toys "R" Us.

Memories came flooding back. Good ones. Garrett was surprised to find the past moments had the power to sting his eyes. His lashes grew wet, and he wiped his arm across them, erasing the tears before they had a chance to bail.

Placing the photo album back in the tote, he thought he saw something move in the corner of the attic. A small thing like a squirrel or a rat. He was immediately on edge—not that he thought the thing (whatever it was) could seriously hurt him, but he didn't want to get bit or scratched and have to deal with rabies or some other injury that would prolong this trip. Furthermore, he didn't want to have to drive anywhere.

You can't drive anywhere, he told himself. *This place won't let you.*

He'd done his best to forget about last night, the bridge. How he'd driven over it, only to find himself driving back over it again and again and again, like the part of a record that kept skipping and playing the same song lyric over and over and over.

It had felt like a dream, that whole sequence. So, he convinced himself that was true—it had been a dream and nothing more. Jean waking up looking better than she ever had was enough to persuade him.

Maybe he'd try the bridge again, later, in daylight. Maybe the never-ending stretch of road was exclusively a nighttime thing.

Garrett shone his flashlight at the corner where the movement had come from. There was nothing there but the plywood sheathing, the framing, and the pink tufts of insulation that poked out from between the joists.

Nothing there at all. No animal.

It was normal to be on edge, he suspected. After everything that had happened this week so far (*Jesus, it's only been three days*), jumping at shadows was forgivable. Hell, *expected.* He was surprised he even had the courage to come up here alone.

He went back to the totes, going through them, more out of curiosity than anything else. He knew they wouldn't keep any of this stuff; sentimental value or not, they just didn't have the space in the car to lug back totes and totes full of crap. And where would they store it anyway? Jean's apartment, from what he understood, was limited to a single room with virtually no storage space, and his Midtown apartment was already packed to capacity. Everything they discovered here would have to go sans a few small items.

He began to push the totes toward the ceiling's egress, the sound of the plastic sliding against the wood canceling out any other potential sounds, especially the rustling of unwanted furry houseguests. Once he got the totes over to the attic stairs, he looked down, trying to see if Jean was at the bottom waiting for him.

She wasn't.

"Jean?" he called. He received no answer. Not that he was expecting one. Jean...Jean was doing her own thing, and whatever that thing was, it was best Garrett didn't know about it.

Those eyes. That EYE.

The colors it held.

Garrett turned his back on the silence below and moved toward the work waiting for him. As soon as he spun around, he saw it again, that flash of movement in the corner, that blur in his periphery that shook his senses, alerted him to the fact that he wasn't alone up here.

But there was nothing visible.

Garrett cleared his throat and did the cliché thing, the thing he'd write in one of his novels if his characters ever faced a similar situation. He asked the empty space, "Hello? Anyone there?"

But he could see there was nothing there—just the attic.

He was alone. That was a fact.

Asking the question felt like a betrayal of his own creativity. After the attic responded with silence, he shimmied his way across the plywood, moving on his butt like a crab with busted legs. When he reached the corner where the movement had come from, he shone his flashlight in the nook where the floor joists met the roof's framing. The insulation had been pulled back some, like something small was creating a nest beneath it.

Probably an animal, Garrett thought, and then decided not to pursue the matter any further. But just as he was about to turn away and resume his afternoon chore, he noticed something carved into the plywood just above his head.

What the...

Two stick figures were scratched into the wood. Above them, a crescent moon. He immediately thought of Jean, her neck, the red mark he'd seen there. Next to the moon, there were stars, five in total. Below the stick figures, Garrett saw the treasure chest, the lid open. The two stick figures' arms were outstretched, and they were joined by an object that Garrett recognized at once—it was the conch.

Just a conch.

Garrett got the impression that the two men were playing tug-of-war with the shell, each vying for position, which was ludicrous because the depiction was merely a few scratches and lines, and how could he possibly gain that much insight from such a simplistic sketch?

I just know, he thought, and then pictured the night he had followed Jean down the beach, when he'd discovered her under the pier, the conch in her hand, the dark juices dripping from her lips, the crescent moon over them doing little to relieve the shadows.

Garrett touched the drawing, ran his fingers along the marred wood as if doing so would give him a greater knowledge of this transaction. He felt an electric buzz thrumming throughout his bones, a charge his senses couldn't adequately process. Had his uncle carved this? The doodle was amateurish enough, which fell in line with his memory of his Uncle Jerry's artistic talents.

Garrett suddenly felt very cold. He shivered and made his

way back to the totes. When he faced the attic stairs, he saw a face staring back at him.

It was Jean.

"I'm here to help," she said with a smile that turned Garrett's blood to ice.

ELEVEN

She couldn't help but laugh. "Are you serious?"

Garrett stalled, tapping his foot on the carpet. Then he pointed to the treasure chest as he puffed out his cheeks. She thought his face might explode from the pressure.

"I'm serious, Jean." He huffed, frustrated. To a certain degree, she understood his attitude. He couldn't comprehend the things she now understood. His brain wasn't built that way, but hers...hers had adapted to the knowledge it could now process. The knowledge she required to *survive*. "This thing... this stupid fucking treasure chest...since we found it, things have gotten...weird. *You've* been weird."

Please explain, she asked with her smile.

"Sleepwalking," he said after her spell of silence. "That night you went under the pier. Like, what was that?"

She blinked rapidly, feigning innocence. "Why, brother, what *ever* in the world are you talking about?"

"Don't do that," he snapped. "Don't play dumb."

But she did. That phony grin never left her face, and she enjoyed every second of this charade.

"What about the other night on the bridge? Huh? You mean to tell me that was normal?"

"What is normal?" she asked. "Normal can mean several different things to several different people."

"You're playing games with me, Jean, and I don't like it. And furthermore, I hate this treasure chest and the stupid shell that's inside of it."

"It's a conch."

"I know it's a fucking conch!" He opened the chest and removed the conch in question, flipping it around his hands, showing off every angle. It was like he was allowing her one last good look at it before he—

Her heart skipped. "You better rethink this before you do anything rash. Something you might regret later."

"Are you threatening me?"

"No, I'm simply issuing a little friendly advice." She winked at him, knowing this was driving up his blood pressure. "If I were threatening you, I'd say something like, 'Don't touch the conch or they will rip open your stomach and eat your spleen.' Now *that* would be a threat."

"You're crazy," he said, and she could tell he meant it, that it wasn't just something he was saying to get under her skin. *You're crazy* hit her soul like a sledgehammer, and she felt dizzy from hearing those two words exit his mouth.

"I'm...not crazy."

"You *are* like mom."

Her heart felt like it could burst, suddenly beating uncontrollably in her chest, lacking any familiar rhythm whatsoever. "You take that back. Right now."

"Or what, Jean? Are you going to eat my spleen too?" He shook his head at her in the most disappointed way. After clicking his tongue, he said, "You're a fucking psycho. You do deserve to be locked up in some padded cell."

In that moment she felt different. Like someone else. Distant from herself, the girl she'd been for the first thirty years of her life.

The rage was in control now. Thirty long years of anger, the result of being ignored, cast aside, belittled, resentment over the lack of attention and care, had finally culminated. A sour taste filled her mouth. Heat flared in her chest; it felt like an oven in there, her heart baking, roasting, catching fire from the match her brother had tossed inside. She launched herself to her feet and it was a graceful move, like an eagle taking flight. As if she had wings and she could soar well above this place. Like she was towering over her brother. Looking down at him. Ready to scratch out his eyes with taloned fingers.

Something in her eyes (*eye*) must have spooked him because he backed up a step. Then two. His face changed. He went from vexed to startled in no time flat.

"What are you doing?" he asked, hiding the alarm in his voice, but not hiding it well enough. "Jean, stop. Sit back down. I'm serious."

"Oh, I didn't realize you were serious," she said. "Please, allow me to take a seat and shut up so you can bore me with more of your candor."

"Jean," he said, continuing to backpedal on his heels as she closed the distance between them. He bumped into the couch and jumped, surprised by the unexpected touch. Quickly, he navigated around it, hopping over the armrest as if he were avoiding the jaws of a vicious gator. Once in the clear and nearing the front door, he put up both hands, pleading. "Stop. This isn't like you. You're acting..."

"What? Out of control? On the edge?" She imagined what she looked like through his eyes, crazy and wild. "Absolutely insane?" Her lower lip twinged.

Garrett maneuvered around the other side of the couch, reaching the hallway opening. She was too slow to catch up to him, not that she necessarily wanted to. If she put her hands on him, there was no telling what she'd do. For a flash, she pictured herself ripping him apart with her bare hands, shredding through his flesh like threadbare clothing. The image excited her, and she was ashamed to admit that, even to herself. But as the shame came and went oh-so-quickly, it was easily replaced by desire.

The burning urge to tear her brother apart, pluck his limbs from his body like a sadistic kiddo might the wings of a beautiful butterfly.

She lunged at him, reaching out with her hands. A sound came from her throat, a foreign noise she did not recognize as her own, but it had risen from her larynx and passed through her vocal cords, so she knew it belonged to her. It was a savage sound, short and guttural. Not human.

"Jean!" Garrett said, and then turned to sprint into the bedroom.

She followed, moving down the hall with a quickness that surprised her. In a second, she was on him, latched onto his back like a child trying to catch a piggyback ride. She got her arms around his throat, legs around his waist, hooking on with all her might. Now that she had him, Jean couldn't decipher where to go from here, what her next move should be. She kept waiting for something to happen, that other part of her that was temporarily in control to invite her on the next leg of this journey. But there was nothing, no voice from that other side. The well of whispers that occasionally accompanied her had dried out.

Then the world was underneath her. Her legs over her. Once gravity balanced itself out, she realized that Garrett had flipped her over by throwing his weight forward. She was on her back, looking up at his red face, his swollen, trembling cheeks, the whites of his bared teeth. Spittle formed on his lips as he tremored.

Then he screamed, a rage-cry-shout that felt like razorblades gliding across her eardrums. The noise sparked something within her, that other part of her, and she screamed back, only her outburst was louder, enough to shake the walls and rattle the trinkets their uncle had kept on the dresser—a picture frame and some loose change—a few items they hadn't thrown out yet. Garrett went stiff, and then he arched back, stepping away from Jean and her new form.

Slowly, Jean rolled over and got on her haunches, prepping herself like an Olympic sprinter waiting for the gunshot to sound off.

In her mind, the shot went off, a crack of thunder overhead. Bolting forward, she readied her fingernails (*claws*) to meet her brother's eyes. She imagined how good it would feel to scoop them out of his skull, squeeze them out like the fruity pulp of a grape skin. She could almost hear the sound of that juicy pop.

And then she saw something flash in front of her, a red blur. The second she realized it was the handle of their uncle's hammer, the lights went out and she was greeted by the unyielding dark that met all dead things.

THE WHOLE THING happened so fast Garrett could barely process the chain of events that had led him here. It had seemed like seconds ago he was pleading for his sister to throw out the chest for all the shit it had caused. Now she was lying before him, head smashed in, blood escaping from the shallow crack on her forehead just below the hairline. In disbelief, he glanced at the hammer, the shiny-silver end now speckled with a deep and dripping red. Then his eyes traveled back to his sister's ruined cranium.

He'd killed her.

One smack. That was all it had taken to end a life.

It almost seemed impossible, like, that wasn't how it was supposed to happen. The human skull was meant to take a beating and survive, right? It happened in movies all the time. But in real life, too. People fell on their heads and survived. They dove into shallow pools headfirst, cracking their skulls on the concrete bottoms. They smashed their heads on the dashboard in awful traffic accidents—survived. Hell, people have been shot in the head and survived.

Jean couldn't be dead. He didn't even hit her that hard.

Evidence suggests differently, he thought, which was a line a detective from his first novel uttered at the scene of a crime, and wasn't it funny how the things he wrote sometimes came back to haunt him?

Garrett paced the room for a beat, unable to process the scene, his emotions, unable to determine what he should do or even where to begin. His chest was so tight he thought his whole body might cave in on itself.

He closed his eyes. Blinked, a lot and rapidly, hoping that when he looked at her again, this lucid dream would end and he'd discover that this whole mess was an illusion, just some trickery of that fucking treasure chest, the conch, because, since they had discovered it, everything post-find was nothing more than a terrible nightmare.

But he saw Jean's head was still bleeding and bleeding badly, the scarlet pool around her head widening, soaking into the plush carpet.

"Fuck," he finally muttered, and it was the only word that seemed adequate for the situation. "Fuck, fuck, fuck. FUCK."

He fell to his knees and dropped the hammer on the blood-soaked carpet. Running his fingers along the wound, he traced the edges of the damage, as if touching them would determine whether the last few minutes were real. But his senses did not betray him.

"Fuck," he said, practically choking on the word this time around.

Jean's open eyes gazed up at him, a vacant and infinite stare that made him feel like something had ruptured in his chest. He did the only thing that seemed logical, and that was to place a palm over her eyelids and shut them forever. At least she couldn't look at him anymore, judge him for all the bad things he'd done over the years, the situations he'd walked out on.

You shoulda walked out on this one, he heard his dead mother saying from her eternal position in the bathtub, a needle sticking out her arm, her jaw slack, her flesh graying. *Shoulda never answered that call from the hospital, no sir.*

Now was not the time to hear his mother's voice, or anyone's for that matter. Now was the time for swift action, to come up with a plan about how to handle the situation. The writer part of his brain tried to figure out how he could spin this, how he could make it look like it was an accident or—even better—a murder. Well, it *was* a murder, but he could stage it like a break-in gone awry, a botched home invasion attempt. Yeah, sure, he could spin it that way. Could make up quite the story to back it all up.

He quickly (*too* quickly) decided to move her body into the closet, thinking he could tell the police that that was where he had found her. That the perpetrators must have killed her and then hid her body in the closet. It wasn't until after he moved her that he realized how dumb it was; not just the moving of her body but also...if a criminal *had* accidentally murdered his sister, he was pretty sure the last thing they'd be concerned with was stashing the body in a place where it would eventually be discovered anyway—they'd be more concerned with getting the fuck elsewhere.

But Garrett wasn't thinking too clearly, his thoughts muddied by the act he'd just carried out, and the knowledge that he was so effective at killing someone. Once she was in the closet, her crumpled, lifeless form nesting on a collection of fallen coats and hangers, he shut the door and turned to the red spot on the carpet about the size of an extra-large dinner plate. For a split second he thought about heading to the pharmacy and getting something to take the stain out because who in their right mind was going to buy a house with a blood stain as big as that on the carpet, and...wasn't that a peculiar thing to think about right now? Selling the goddamn house when his dead sister was sitting in a closet, no more than a few feet away?

His mind raced with wacky thoughts, too fast for him to cling to any one in particular.

Instead of doing something, he backed himself into the corner. Back against the wall, he slid until his bottom reached the floor. He tucked his head between his knees, sobbing uncontrollably, his entire body shuddering with each outburst. Saliva dripped from his open mouth and his sinuses opened, releasing plenty of nasally discharge. In no time at all, his jeans were soaked at the knees.

After five minutes of purging the emotional well, he leaned his head back and stared at the door, having no idea how he was going to spin this, *if* he was going to spin this at all. *You're going to jail, asshole. For murdering your sister.* He could see the headlines now: "Hack Crime Writer Murders Sister in Cold Blood." He could also see his agent making it rain with all the royalties he'd get from the book-sale spike post-conviction, because let's face it; who wouldn't want to read a crime novel penned by a convicted murderer? He could almost smell the public discourse and arguments that would dominate social media, bringing into question the moral and ethical obligation of the publisher to pull the books from publication.

A thud ripped him from these false futures. At first he thought it was his own heart that made the sound, like this was Poe's classic tale come to life, but after a second he knew the sound had come from outside his own body. The front door? He couldn't be sure.

Garrett tuned his ear to the dreadful silence.

Waited.

The thud happened again; it was inside the room.

The door.

The closet door.

Now his heart made a noise inside him, a thunderous boom that pinched every nerve in his body.

Another bang. More forceful this time. Something inside needing to get out.

"Fuck," he said again, somberly this time. He wiped his nose and hunched forward, unable to comprehend what his ears were allowing him to hear.

The door handle jiggled.

Another knock sounded.

The door handle turned again. Since it was the closet door, it couldn't have been locked, so Garrett figured the hand didn't have the strength to turn the knob.

That's because she's dead, he thought, *and the dead don't have the strength to operate door handles.*

"J-Jean?" he whimpered. "Th-that you?"

He waited for a response, and the moment passed without any sound. No knocking, no corpse within trying to release itself from this shallow tomb stuffed with clothes and shoes and inconsequential things.

Then: *"Gar?"*

His heart broke just then. Shattered.

"Gar? Help me?"

Slowly, he crawled across the room and over to the closet door, wondering when he was going to wake up from this continuous nightmare.

"How..." he started to ask, but then stopped himself. Was he really going to ask her how she was alive, as if she'd know? It didn't matter, the how or the why; it only mattered that she *was* still alive and that he wasn't a murderer.

"Help me, Gar," she said again, her voice deeper than before. *"I need you to help me. Can you do that?"*

He wasn't speaking to his sister. The tone of her voice was all off, too happy. Too content with what had just taken place here.

"Yes," he croaked.

"Good. I need you to bring it to me."

Excitement in her voice. He hated it. Almost as much as he hated the fear in his own voice, that prominent tremble that punctuated each spoken word.

"Bring you wuh-what?"

A pause, the worst kind of silence, long and knowing something terrible was waiting on the other end of it.

"*You know what,*" she said in a resonant warble, like an old cassette seconds before getting swallowed by a faulty tape deck. "*The conch. Bring it.*"

He looked to the door, his exit, his way out, and then back to the closet. It was as if there was no barrier between them, as if she could see directly into his brain, the thoughts that dwelled there.

"*I know what you're thinking. But trust me. You can't run from this, not this time. Bring the conch and all of this goes away. We can fix this. Together. Don't be frightened.*"

"The conch is bad," he said, feeling confident in that claim.

"*Oh,*" she said, her voice meant to reassure, but the childish pitch only made Garrett more afraid. "*Oh, Garrett—no. The conch is magic. It has the ability to make all the bad things go away. Isn't that what you want?*"

It was. But he wished there was another way, a more *natural* solution. Just thinking about touching the conch made him queasy.

"It's changing you."

"*For the better.*"

He sat there cross-legged for what seemed like an eternity, but then he decided she was right—there was no running from this. He'd made a terrible mistake, an impulsive decision that he now had to deal with, and what choice did he have? It was run or face this thing head-on, whatever they were dealing with.

The conch.

Bring it.

"I'll be right back," he said.

HE SHUFFLED into the living room feeling like he'd been the one hit on the head with a hammer. Dizzy and disoriented, the world blurred near the edges. He guessed killing someone—smashing their head in—had side effects and these altered states were just some of them.

Before he located the conch, he saw his laptop resting on the edge of the table, tilted sideways at an odd angle for someone expecting to type on it, and perhaps more alarming—it wasn't where he had last left it. He didn't remember taking it out of the office. But here it was. In front of him. Word processor opened, his document for *Killing Spaces* stared him in the face. Only...

It wasn't the manuscript he'd remember adding a few hundred words to earlier that morning.

In fact, it wasn't the manuscript at all.

He checked the entire document, what should have been an impressive twelve thousand words. Using the Tools tab and pulling up the word count, he saw the document contained less than two thousand, all of them the same word typed over and over again—LEAVE. In all caps. Period after each one-word command. Pages and pages full of the lone message.

LEAVE.

LEAVE.

LEAVE.

LEAVE. LEAVE. LEAVE. LEAVE.

A bang went off in his chest, hot like a July firecracker. He thought he'd been punched by some invisible spirit but then realized it was just his heartbeat. Thunder in his ear. Sauna-like heat beneath his collar.

LEAVE.

He wasn't going to do that. Was he?

He couldn't.

It wouldn't let them.

Tripp's Isle wouldn't. Or at least, whatever was inside his sister wouldn't. The invisible monster that was changing her. Mutating her. Making her become something she wasn't meant to become.

He grabbed the conch off the counter and forced himself back into the bedroom.

There, he opened the closet door just enough for the conch to fit inside. Before he could drop the shell to his sister, two hands left the darkness within and reached for the object. Garrett was so shocked by their appearance that he almost let go of the conch. An audible gasp left his mouth. The shell's chalky surface slipped from his fingers, but the hands, covered in a dark scaly rash and displaying lifted fingernails that looked smashed by hammers themselves, were there to catch the conch before it could fully escape Garrett's grip.

No *thank you*. No *good boy*. No commentary on the good deed whatsoever.

Just a brief moment of silence that was soon interrupted by the wet slurping sounds coming from within the closet.

SHE COULD HARDLY REMEMBER what happened. It felt like a flash. She was standing before Garrett one moment (doing what, who knew?) and then there was pitch black. Next thing she knew, her eyes were open, staring into an expanse of dominating darkness. Like, deep-space dark. Several seconds later, shadows formed vague images and she could see the rectangular outline of the door, the frame of light coming through from the other side. Seconds after that, the door handle took shape.

Too weak to escape on her own, she called out to her brother.

He answered. Eventually. Then dragged her out of the closet and into the center of the room. He helped her to a seated position next to a spherical stain on the carpet, wet, red, and dark. She got dizzy from the realization that it was her blood. Or was it hers? If not, then whose?

She didn't know.

She didn't know much anymore.

Except for what the whispers told her.

"I'M SO SORRY, JEAN," he said for the eleventh time. "I'm so goddamn sorry."

She smiled at him, and there was something in that smile that suggested it wasn't Jean at all behind those eyes, but whatever she had released from the treasure chest. That other presence that had taken his sister hostage.

Garrett stared at her bad eye, the one that did not belong to her.

"Forgive me?" he asked, examining the wound. It looked much better than it had before he stashed her in the closet. Cleaner, neater, smaller. It had healed at some exponential rate. The only explanation was something supernatural. That, or he was losing his goddamn mind and the psychotic break had him imagining the most terrible things. Her hands had reverted to their natural color, the diseased rash gone, no evidence it had ever been there to start with. He glanced at the red stain and saw it had shrunk since his last view. Which was impossible. But his eyes did not deceive him.

Evidence suggests differently.

"I forgive you," she said, wrapping her thin, normal arms around his neck, pulling him closer.

He buried his nose in her shoulder, inhaled the salty scent of the sea, the smoky scent of burning stars.

"I forgive you, brother," she whispered. "Always and forever."

TWELVE

Garrett cleaned the dishes while Jean sat on the couch. He kept glancing over his shoulder every minute or so just to make sure his eyes weren't playing a prank on him. Over the last four hours, her wound had diminished and, currently, there was no mark on her forehead near the hairline whatsoever.

It was fucking gone. The blood stain, too.

Disappeared. Evaporated. *Poof,* a magic trick.

He convinced himself he'd imagined the whole thing, though it was difficult to persuade his brain that everything he'd witnessed in the bedroom had been a mere figment of his imagination.

Then again, he'd convinced himself of worse things.

Jean continued to watch television as if the chain of events from earlier had never happened, cackling at the sitcom, whatever was playing on one of the two basic cable channels that came through Uncle Jerry's outdated television set. Between each obnoxious laugh she shoved a handful of popcorn in her mouth. The crunching between her teeth was so loud in Garrett's ears that he cringed.

Maybe he was the damaged one, not her.

Whatever was happening, it wasn't right. Whatever she'd done under the pier, whatever she'd sipped from the conch—that smelly ichor—it was changing her, and Garrett couldn't sit idly by while it...

What? Made her better? Filled her with happiness and hope, transfused a little joyful radiance in her life?

Why would he want to take that away?

Because...it's evil. It's changing her but it's also taking something from her, too.

Garrett had no evidence to back this up, but he'd seen this scenario play out in books and movies before. An invading demonic presence never just gave its host eternal satisfaction in exchange for nothing, no—it always took something for itself. There was always a trade. A deal in place, a symbiotic relationship built on dangerous accords. And it was always costly for the host, *deadly* in most cases.

Garrett swallowed his trepidation. It was hard to fight something when he had no idea what he was dealing with. Or where to begin. He wondered if Uncle Jerry knew what the chest stored inside, if he knew anything about it at all or if it was just something he had found and was planning to explore at some later date. A date that never came because he died.

Drowned. In the sea.

Garrett was beginning to suspect that Uncle Jerry's cause of death might not be what the coroner logged on the official death certificate.

Garrett was beginning to suspect a lot of things.

Cautiously he entered the room, the way one might approach if they needed to walk around a sleeping bear. He cleared his throat. "*Ahem.* Jean?"

She paused her sitcom marathon, gracing him with her attention. He could almost see the happiness sparkling in her eyes. "Yes, brother?"

He swallowed what felt like a mouthful of beach pebbles. "I...I went to go get you some aspirin, you know, for your headache...and I just realized I threw out all of Uncle Jerry's medications, even the basic stuff, you know, when we first got here." He laughed nervously through his teeth. "Couldn't be too cautious, you know."

"Oh, I know." Her eyebrows jumped up and down. "I appreciate you looking out for me, brother."

"Yeah...so, anyway, I was just thinking that I should head to the pharmacy, to pick up a few things. Plus...I'm really craving ice cream. Do you want ice cream?"

He felt like he was asking a parent permission to hang out with friends on a school night. She stared at him like a parent unsure whether to trust said kid's solemn swear to be home by curfew.

"Sure," she finally said, grinning. "I'd love some. Pistachio if they have it."

He nodded. "Excellent." Grabbing his keys off the top of the television, he added, "I won't be long."

"I sure hope not," she replied, and the way she said it sent chilly cascades down his spine.

THE MOMENT he left the house, a shot of adrenaline coursed through his veins. He was free. He could go anywhere, do anything, and no one could stop him. Jean couldn't stop him.

Once he reached the car and opened the door, he took one last look at the house, the blue glow radiating from the television set. She didn't follow him. Nor did the thing that now occupied her. The thing that made him see things, things that were not there. Illusions. That was what they were. Tricks of the mind. But he was free of them now. Free of them and the responsibilities he'd agreed upon before coming here. Free of his sister's delusions, her illness.

At least, he thought he was.

He sped toward the bridge, accelerating to a speed that even he thought was a little dangerous considering the short roads and many turns he would have to take. Doing sixty-five in a residential was dicey, but then again—he couldn't be far enough away from everything he'd just experienced.

I'm going to drive over that bridge, and if it takes me back here, if I'm stuck in that goddamn loop, I'm just going to keep driving until I run out of gas.

Then I'll walk back to New York.

He gunned for the bridge, topping out at eighty-five. There were no cars in front of him, nothing there to impede his exit save for the world itself, the illusions that Tripp's Isle had shown him.

Come on, you bastard. Come on.

He didn't even care that he had left his laptop behind, the manuscript that may or may not have been deleted. He suspected Jean (in her altered new form) dumped the file into the trash bin and erased it from the hard drive. It wasn't her fault. He couldn't blame her.

The chest.

The conch.

Uncle Jerry.

If anyone was to blame, it was their uncle for dying, leaving them the house, and opening the door for them to get caught up in this calamitous sequence of events.

Fuck Uncle Jerry, Garrett thought. *Fuck this entire family.*

He sped toward the bridge's apex, and once he crossed it, a cool rush came over him, an almost euphoric wash that broke over him and scattered across his body, infiltrating every nerve. Every cell within him was suddenly alive, stricken with a simultaneous injection of both pleasure and pain. He suspected he knew what this new feeling was, and when he reached the bottom of the bridge, the flat stretch of road that led to the next highway, the one road that would take him far, far away from here, he confirmed the theory to be true.

It was the sense of being released.

Of being truly free.

He merged with the highway and set his sights on home, New York City, where he belonged, and where he would never leave ever again, under any circumstance whatsoever.

JEAN WAS WATCHING TELEVISION, joining in with the sitcom's uproarious laugh track, when she caught something moving in her periphery. A darting shadow. She was slow to react, craning her head in the direction of the house's west interior wall, and saw nothing but the painting that hung there.

Nothing.

Nothing to worry about, nothing to panic over. No intruding presence, no whispers. All was good, okie-dokie, and Jean was relieved that since the blackout in the closet, not a single weird thing had happened to her. No dizzy spells or moments of displacement. That mindfuck feeling of being on a boat and getting rocked by a tumultuous sea, the one that had plagued her all week since their arrival, was all but gone.

For the first time since they had crossed the bridge into Tripp's Isle, she felt pretty okay.

The painting attracted her eyes again. Her entire body felt drawn to it; she could feel that convincing pull, that magnetic force summoning her off the couch and toward the wall. A few footfalls later, she was in front of the painting, scoping out the vast black ocean, running her fingers along the whitecaps, the frame of the small fishing boat. As she examined the brush-strokes and other nuances an ordinary person might gloss over, she spotted something in the artwork she hadn't before—yards from the boat, beyond the two fishermen aboard, a head was floating in the water, depicted from the nose up. Strands of wet hair dangled around those strange eyes, disappearing beneath the obsidian surface. But it was the eyes that stood out the most, their assorted colors and size difference; Jean recognized the shade of the right eye, the one she'd viewed in the mirror before, and when she concentrated on the painting, her own right eye gave a gentle twitch.

What felt like liquid ice leaked across her shoulders, spreading down the small of her back.

Then the whispers restarted their terrible chorus, filling her ears and smothering the silence. She spun around, sensing something lurking in the corners of the room. Before her eyes noticed the shape near the doorway, she saw the television show had been interrupted, ruined by layers upon layers of static interference and squiggly lines that looked like demented rainbows.

But it was the hunched form near the door that gripped her attention now. At first she thought it was her own shadow, long and stretched, but that didn't make much sense because she stood a considerable distance away from the new presence and the lights in the room weren't positioned in a way to project herself that far. No, it was a new form, a figure, another *person*.

Not a person, she thought, running her eyes over the intruder, the dark nature of its appearance. Jean's eyes flicked from the painting, the head bobbing in the water, back over to the huddling guest. The scraggly hair, the two different color eyes. It was the same thing from the painting come to life. It was standing in front of her, and...

It looked like her.

Jean.

A copy.

Though, this version of her was covered from head to toe in dark scales, the pale, fish-belly skin weaved throughout, textured like marble. The figure rose from its crouched position, the dark version of Jean's spine straightening. *Dark Jean.* This replica was much taller than her, by more than a foot. It did not speak—instead, it leered at her for several seconds before its lips stretched in a mischievous grin. It beckoned her forth with its eyes...its *eye*, the colors within swirling like melting prisms, a hypnotic façade that left Jean feeling drowsy. Lightheaded. Empty. Impossibly tired, like she could fall asleep standing up, and too lethargic to place herself on the couch where she could rest for a spell. Looking into this creature that held very similar features to her own was draining, depleting her energy. Like staring at it was taking something away from her.

Dark Jean raised a hand, her index finger sticking straight up while her other fingers curled, forming a tight fist. The index finger waved slowly, back and forth, like a worm succumbing to death's onset.

Follow, a voice whispered, rising above all others.

Dreamily, Jean followed. Out into the dark. Down the walk. Across the beach.

Where *they* were waiting for her.

THIRTEEN

Garrett pulled into the pharmacy's parking lot, parked, and sat there for some indeterminate amount of time. He smacked himself in the head over and over again, screamed at his reflection in the rearview, and then drove his knuckles into the radio, hard enough to leave them sore after the short-lived rush of numbness had worn off.

"FUCK!" he shouted, not caring if anyone passing by overheard him. Now that he was back in civilization, there were other people walking around, heading in and out of the pharmacy.

He didn't know why he had stopped. He could have easily kept going. Could have driven right by the fucking place and been that much closer to home.

But he couldn't fight the feeling that all of this was wrong.

LEAVE, the message on his computer had read. And he had listened. But now that he was here, he realized how wrong it all was. How he'd left once before, several years ago, and where had that gotten them?

Mom was dead, sis was well on her way to joining her, and

oh, look at Garrett Pryce—he was doing just fine, thank you very much. Not wealthy but certainly not poor, and things were trending in the right direction for a modest, successful writing career.

Meanwhile, anyone who shared the same blood was dead or dying.

Isn't that nice?

"FUCK!" he screamed again, pounding the dashboard, nearly cracking a knuckle in the process, but he didn't care—the pain was almost satisfying. The violence—in some odd way—soothed him. Brought him down. Evened him out. Like smoking a cigarette or having a beer after a bad fucking day.

He tore himself out of the front seat, walked the length of the parking lot, and passed through the front door. He headed straight for the pharmacy's counter. The assistant behind the plexiglass wall greeted him.

"Here to pick up a script for my sister," he said nervously. He felt jittery, a something-bad-is-about-to-happen hunch keeping him on edge. "Jean Pryce."

The assistant clacked away on the keyboard. "Should be ready in five minutes."

"Appreciate it," he said, and then moved down the nearest aisle, immediately going for the small section of popular paperbacks.

Of course, his first novel *wasn't* among them. More popular genres dominated the selections, romance and mainstream thrillers, police procedurals and YA science fiction. Sure, there was King and Koontz, an Anne Rice classic, but there were no other dark fiction authors represented. But it didn't matter. For some reason, just being among the books, the collective new-glue smell and ink fresh off the printer, was enough to bring his emotions to a simmer. Bring him back down the same way the violence had only moments ago.

"You always were a fucking nerd," a familiar voice said, and that voice hit him like being sucker-punched while blindfolded. He turned and nearly lost all control of his bodily functions. An intense flare of pain wrecked his chest. If he had been in worse shape, he might have thought this was the prelude to a minor heart attack. "What? Seen a ghost or something?"

Garrett could barely find his voice, took him about thirty seconds to locate the single world that had been on the precipice of his tongue the moment the voice echoed through his ear canals.

"Mom?" he said, and then watched the woman turn up a vicious smile.

───

JEAN'S BODY was on fire; not literally, of course. Invisible flames licked the surface of her skin, burning her up like a high fever. A glossy sheen of sweat layered every inch of her. The unexpected humidity wasn't the cause of it. Neither were the torches that circled her.

Torches?

She observed the length of the beach before her, wondering exactly how she had gotten here. None of it made much sense. A second ago she was watching television. She vaguely remembered glancing over at Uncle Jerry's wall where the painting hung. She remembered that...

And that was it.

She didn't remember leaving the couch or taking a stroll down the block and over the dunes.

The torches—twelve of them, she assessed—controlled the darkness with a glow that reminded her of pale tangerines. Next to each torch, a hooded figure stood guard. The twelve shapes held onto the bamboo sticks, not budging an inch, even when Jean came to. For a second, Jean doubted their authenticity, chalking up their appearance to more of the fever-dream qualities Tripp's Isle had adopted since their arrival. Since the medicine started. Since whatever that ER doctor prescribed. Once she thought back on this, the sequence of events leading up until this moment, it had all begun once she got on the island and started taking the pills. The dreams. The walks. Those chronological discrepancies.

The pills...

Disoriented, her vision skipped from robed figure to robed figure, waiting for one of them to explain themselves, and the situation at hand. The figures remained statue-still, as if leaving their post was apt to get them killed.

She looked for an exit. Last she checked, her legs were still attached, and she still had the ability to run. As soon as she turned and eyed the dunes behind her, she noticed two figures were approaching, holding each other's hands. One was garbed in a black robe; however, his hood was pushed back, revealing his face to the outside world. It was a face she may have recognized, like an old neighbor she might have had years back but couldn't place the name or where she knew him from. He was older, not quite elderly, and wore the face of someone who'd been in this situation before. Calm. Tranquil. He walked with a confident gait. As he stepped into the torchlight, she saw his pockmarked cheeks, his sunburnt forehead that was peeling in spots. The smile on his face made her gag.

The woman next to him was wearing a white robe, the hood

also pushed back, resting around her neck. This was a face Jean recognized immediately, and when she laid eyes on the woman, she almost shouted. Cursed. Spat.

"Hello, darling." The woman's stretching grin caused bile to creep up Jean's throat. "It's so great to see you again," Patti said.

"MOM," Garrett said, his heart pumping frantically, like a drunk dancer with no sense of rhythm. "This can't be..."

"What?" she asked indignantly. A cigarette stuck to her dry, cracked lips. Grunting, she lit up the smoke in the center of the pharmacy. A foggy stream unfurled toward the ceiling's air conditioner vents. "You got a problem?" Sucking in another drag, she eyed him. Cocked her brow. Blew out another huge gust of smoke, a rolling cloud that dissolved when it hit his face. Even though he was fairly certain the image before him was not truly there, he could still smell the ashy, second-hand exhalation, and a whiff of liquor strong as rubbing alcohol in the aftermath of the smoky assault.

"You're not real," he said, blinking, trying to scrub away the vision.

"Well, no shit, Garrett. What the fuck did you think? I'm a fucking corpse, shithead. Last time I checked, we didn't get up and walk around. Maybe in one of your shitty-ass books, but not in real life, bub."

He closed his eyes and smacked himself in the mouth. Several times, hard enough to hurt. Shaking his whole body as if clearing a chill from his spine, he opened his eyes, hoping the self-cruelty had worked and cleared the mirage before him.

"Sir?" the pharmacist called from the counter. "Can I...uh... help you?"

Garrett realized what a man smacking himself in the mouth and talking to his dead mother in front of the toothpaste products must have looked like.

"I'm okay," he said, forcing a slight smile. Beads of sweat leaked from his sideburns. His armpits became humid saunas of flesh and hair. When he spun around, facing the section his dead mother had just been, he expected to find her gone, vanished along with the last memory of her. But she wasn't. Still present, Elaine Allen-Pryce exhaled a huge plume of smoke. She looked more dead than she had only moments ago, her flesh now gray and decaying in sections, pockets of loose, dangly skin revealing the putrid muscle beneath, yellow and bubbling with pus. He noticed a hole in her cheek that hadn't been there previously, an earthworm sliding through the gap and falling onto the floor. The worm hit the ground with a wet splat and crawled near Garrett's shoe. Even though it wasn't real, he still stepped away, not wanting the goddamn thing to touch him.

"You look like you've seen a ghost," she said, arranging her lips in a wry, evil-stepmother grin.

He wasn't so sure how to respond, so he kept quiet.

She shook her head the way she always had when he had disappointed her. If he came home from school too late or forgot to take out the trash after dinner or clean his room every Saturday morning, that was the look he'd receive. Most of the time, a single disapproving nod would accompany that little twist of the lips. Both filled him with so much ire, then and now.

"I hope you're happy, Garrett. Really. Hope you're proud of yourself." She tsked him. Her lower lip quivered. "Pathetic."

"Fuck you."

She squinted. Chortled. His anger seemed to delight her. "Why'd you do it?"

"Do what?"

"You know what, you little shit."

(*the bathtub, Mother, her skin graying, foam bubbling on her lips, body convulsing*)

"You know goddamn well," she added. "You left me there."

He wasn't startled by this accusation. "You were..."

(*eyes open, searching, lips, barely open but trying to speak, trying to beg, trying to*)

"...dead," he said, and he felt something inside him come apart. Tears emerged, spilling down his cheeks in a rush.

"No," she said, still smiling, still sounding excited by the conflict within him. "No, you're wrong and you know it. Remember, Garrett. Remember what you did..."

(*her eyes, blinking, alive, pleading*)

"You were dead," he said firmly.

"*Help me,*" Garrett's mother said as if mocking someone pleading for their life, but it wasn't mockery; it was what she'd said to him that night, the night he had found her. "*Help me, Garrett.*"

Tears came without any restraint, and Garrett bowed his head. The strength in his legs weakened and he crumbled to his knees.

She bent down, reveling in the chance to chirp directly in his ear. "*Oh, Garrett. Please help me,*" she whispered. "*Please, please, please. Save me. Save your mother.*"

"Shut up."

"And what did you do?" She snarled. Spat in his face. He felt her (*not real*) saliva run down his cheek. "What did you do to your poor, poor mother? Your sick mother that just needed a little help?"

"I said shut up," he barked between two heavy sobs. "Shut the fuck up."

"You left."

(*the needle in the vein, pulling the skin, mother too weak to take it out, the tears spilling down her face merging with the overflowing bath water, her eyes going dark, going cold, going vacant, that pleading stare stuck in its ceaseless state*)

"You found me," she continued, "alive and there was enough time to save me. The paramedics could have gotten there, administered NARCAN. They could have brought me back."

(*Garrett backing out of the bathroom while his mother called to him, called his name, called for help, called for him to dial emergency services*)

"You killed me, Garrett," his mother said sharply. She might as well have jabbed a dagger through his heart.

Garrett stopped crying and was able to control his emotions, the sadness and regret now careening toward anger, a hatred that knew no bounds. "I didn't kill you."

"Yes, you did. You didn't save me, and you could have. That's the same as injecting the needle yourself."

"No," he said, "you were already dead. Not physically, but mentally. You were gone."

"People can get better, Garrett. People can change. Lots of people overdose, die and come back, change themselves, their lives, and live on to become productive members of society. Good parents. Teachers for those who've traveled similar paths and made the same mistakes. Who knows what could have happened if you hadn't abandoned me." She kissed his forehead. The smoke-scent was stronger now, and he could taste the chalky-ash flavor on his lips. "Who were you to choose death for me?"

A sharp pain bit into Garrett's chest. "You wouldn't have changed. You were...like rotten fruit. There was no way to reverse what you did to us."

"Did to you? What did I do to you? I wasn't a horrible mother. I provided. Kept a roof over your head. You never went hungry. Never slept a night outside your own bed. That's better than most people can say."

"You think that's okay? That you not being there was okay? Just because we had food and a bed to sleep in? You have no idea what you put us through, the mental torment." He shook his head, allowing the rage to settle, cool like molten lava. "Plus...when I left you that day, I wasn't killing you. I was saving *her*..."

"Who?"

"Who?" He laughed humorlessly. "Your fucking daughter."

Elaine scoffed. "Saving her from what?"

"From *you*," he said. "But that said...I *was* wrong. And I *am* sorry." He couldn't stop the flood of tears. "You...you're right, I should have tried...to save you. Find you help. I shouldn't have left. At the time I thought it was the right thing to do, but...it wasn't. I know that now, and Christ—I'm so fucking sorry."

"You wanted me to die. You've always wanted me dead."

"That's not true."

"But it is." Her fingers danced along his scalp. She brushed back some loose strands of hair that were dangling close to his eyes. "You hated me. I wasn't perfect, not even close, but I was a good mother to you."

"I'm so sorry," he said. His anger had dried back up again,

and he was weeping now. Kneeling and crying and holding a box of toothpaste against his cheek.

A small crowd had gathered around him. He heard someone say they'd dialed 9-1-1. The pharmacist stood in the center of the group, looking down at him.

Garrett blinked, used his shoulder to dry his eyes. When the blurry filter over his vision cleared away, he saw the group—six strangers and the one employee—all looking at him through sad, empathetic eyes.

His mother was not among them.

She had vanished.

"Someone is coming to get you help, sir," the pharmacist said.

Garrett dropped the box of toothpaste on the ground and fished out his phone. There was a message sitting in the inbox from an unknown number. One word: LEAVE.

Garrett got to his feet and turned for the door. He hustled out, ignoring the requests from the employee and the patrons to stay put and wait for help. That *they* were on the way and things would be fine once *they* got here.

They. Help.

They were right. Help was on the way. And things would get better.

FOURTEEN

Jean was at a loss. She couldn't find the right words to say, the correct questions to ask so this would all make sense. She continued to focus on Patti, the woman's radiant face lit by the waxing gibbous moon that seemed much too close to the planet to be real. The other robed attendees remained rooted at their posts, as if awaiting instruction from the newcomers.

"Jean," Patti finally said when she and her husband finished their stroll, positioning themselves about ten feet away from her. "I'm so happy you're here."

"What is this?" she asked, her lungs feeling short of breath. "Who are you people?"

Patti and Peter exchanged glances, smiles. Their eyes twinkled with a colorless, cosmic glow, as if they were from the same luminous gas that made up the stars.

Peter was the first to open his mouth. "The sea," he said, folding his hands in front of him, "is such a strange place. The fact is, we know less about the depths of the ocean than we do about our own galaxy."

That couldn't be true, but Jean wasn't in the arguing mood. Plus, she knew nothing of the sea and the stars. "Why are you telling me this?"

"You've been given a gift, Jean," Patti said, clapping her hands together as if celebrating some proud accomplishment. Like this was a party for some momentous occasion in Jean's life. "The conch, it's chosen you. It's spoken to you. You've been elected as its chief listener."

Jean's heart froze. A glacial stream coursed through her veins.

"Your uncle," Peter said. "He heard the call too."

"The call?"

"The whispers, sweetheart," Patti explained. "Throughout the history of Tripp's Isle, it was always believed that certain people shared a special connection with the sea and the stars, that this place sat on a threshold of some other reality. An alien place. That the island was a space that wasn't quite part of one world or another, that it rested between two separate realities."

"Like the space between the sea and the stars," Peter said, putting a hand on his wife's shoulder. "Few people have admitted to hearing the whispers. When your uncle and I found that chest out in the ocean, he started hearing them. After that... well, let's just say he could not handle the gift that had been bestowed upon him."

"It killed him?" Jean asked.

"Something like that, darling," Patti said, bowing her head as if paying respects to the dead man.

"Drove him to madness," Peter said. "He tried to destroy the chest and the secret inside, tried to hide it from us...but..." He frowned.

"We would not be denied what our people have searched eons for," Patti finished. Her eyes glimmered with determination. "Our families have scoured the ocean, the available depths for that artifact, that piece that binds us to that *other* reality. And we found it."

"And your uncle wanted to take that away from us," Peter said, his tongue sharp with bitter disappointment.

"Oh god," Jean said, finally understanding. The chest and the conch within may have driven her uncle to madness, but it was not responsible for his death. "It was you."

Patti and Peter's elation rose, their lips stretching farther and farther across their sun-tanned faces.

"Jesus Christ," Jean muttered, shuddering.

"Christ likely won't be of any help to you, dearie," said Patti, proudly sporting a cheery grin.

"You were hoping we'd come." Jean fought back tears. "Did you make him do it? Did you make him leave the house in our name?"

"We knew he had relatives," Patti told her. "I wasn't lying to your brother about that. Jerry talked about you two quite a bit. Only relatives he had left, he told us. The house was left to you all by his own doing, though he did try to get that changed, tried to leave you two off and out of it once he found out...well, once he discovered whatever that chest showed him."

"We stopped him before he could do such a thing," Peter admitted.

Jean put a hand over her chest like that would slow her rapidly beating heart. "Holy fuck."

"Indeed."

"Your brother," Patti said, her proud eyes beaming, "I knew

he'd take the coward's way out. Knew he'd leave you in the end, high and dry. I have to say, I am quite astonished it took him so long. Thought the first sign of trouble and—" She smacked her lips together, making a snappy popping sound, "—off he'd go."

"Fuck you," Jean spat. "Fuck you, fuck all of you!"

"Oh, that's no way to speak, purdy young thang like yourself." Patti giggled. "Now...we have to do some things to you that, likely, you might not be in the mood for doing...so, you can either cooperate with us...or we can *make* you cooperate."

Jean felt the presence of two tall shadows at her back. She didn't need to turn around to see their hulking forms standing over her. Jean glanced down the beach, toward the pier. Someone else was walking toward them. A shadowy form slicked with darkness, a luminous thread outlining its human shape.

"What is it?" Patti asked.

Jean ignored her, kept staring at the approaching figure.

"Is it..." Patti grew excited by the prospect. Jean wondered if they could see what she was seeing. "Is it a visitor? Our guide to the other side?"

"Shut up," Peter told her. "We don't want to scare it away."

Jean didn't think there was anything this approaching form was afraid of. It marched toward her with an overwhelming sense of confidence. When it got nearer, entering the outer rim where the torchlight and midnight dark conjoined, Jean could see exactly what the form was, the appearance it had taken.

Copied, Jean thought.

Jean's dark replica stepped into the fiery glow of the torchlit circle. Jean gazed into the mirage's obsidian eyes as it grew closer. It stopped about six feet away. Jean could smell the ocean on her, the briny tang imbued with the night. The replica's body was soaked, still dripping. The wet hair that fell at its shoulders was much darker than Jean's natural color. There were other subtle differences too, specifically the anatomical proportions. Longer arms that seemed to hang past the knees. Its head sat crookedly on the neck, like it had been broken and never healed correctly. Its bare feet were significantly arched, and the toes protruded out at odd, twisted angles, like someone had taken a hammer and smashed them until the bones were broken, fragmented in places.

"Is it here?" Patti asked, frantically searching the darkness like she'd lost her kid in a supermarket. "Is the shepherd ready to guide us to the other side?"

Peter's elastic grin expanded. "It's here. I can feel it."

"You can't see it?" Jean asked, fending off another spell of lightheadedness.

"No," Patti whispered, as if trying to avoid spooking a cute critter that had stumbled into her backyard. "No, only you can. What's it saying?"

Jean stared at the shadowy shape, watching its misshapen head tilt to the side as if it didn't understand its own presence here. She couldn't decipher what the thing wanted from her, or if it wanted anything at all. Was it just merely curious? Was it amused? Was there any desire to interact with humanity? Or did it come solely to observe?

Jean couldn't gauge its intent. She watched as the thing moved closer, shortening the gap between them.

The whispers in her head buzzed as Jean's copy reached for her, her hand. As its clammy flesh grazed her fingers, an electric buzz reverberated throughout Jean's entire body. Like she'd thrown herself on a nest of live wires. The charge traveled through every bone, leaving her tingly and numb and feeling oh-so-elevated. In the seconds that followed, nothing else mattered —every worry, every failed hope and dream, every single problem inside Jean Pryce's head suddenly dissipated, and the emptiness that filled her felt like she'd won some euphoric lottery.

Dark Jean grabbed Jean's hand, a forceful grip that raised all the red flags. Jean felt her fingers getting crushed under the applied pressure. The incredible swell of pain was jolting. She tried to break away, retract her hand, but this invader from another world held on, did not let up, not a fraction. It squeezed until Jean heard and felt something pop—her bones breaking like thin tree bark. Snapping, crackling.

Pain. Too much to bear.

Then the figure leaned in and kissed her, its lips sucking against her own. Wet. Passionate. Perhaps the best kiss she'd ever experienced. It was the way Jean would have kissed a lover, had she ever truly loved someone. If she could ever find someone to love her back the way she loved, if she could find someone to put up with her quirks, her thoughts, the things she said when the bad times came, when she couldn't control the stuff that came from her mouth. The words, the insults, the negativity that flowed during those dark periods of mental unrest.

As Dark Jean's lips lingered on hers, the lightheadedness was amplified, and the world began to turn before her at a frenzied pace, dimming as it spun.

THE SECOND GARRETT stepped foot in the house, he knew something had changed. The progress they had made in Uncle Jerry's living room had been undone. There was stuff everywhere. It looked like someone had lugged the garbage from the curb back into the house and dumped it across the room. Trash littered the ground, torn pieces of paper and tattered clothing. Garrett shuffled forward as if stepping across some impossible dreamscape, tentatively stepping foot in the alien world in fear that it would be his last.

Who did this?

The evidence pointed to one person and one person only —*Jean*. In Garrett's mind he pictured his sister having a complete mental collapse and lugging the trash back into the house, tossing it everywhere, laughing like a lunatic as she spread the refuse evenly throughout the room.

Leave.

He wanted to. He wanted to convince himself that this was a mistake, that he shouldn't have come back here.

But every time he heard that word, that phantom voice whispering *leave, leave, leave* repeatedly, he pictured his mother's dead face, her eyes alive but only for a few more moments as the poison ran through her veins, slowly ushering her over to the other side where one dreams forever.

He wasn't going to leave, not this time.

In the center of the garbage, he saw something red sticking out of the pile, about nine inches long, a cherry-colored handle. He moved for it, pulled it free. The shiny metal hammerhead gleamed at him despite the frail lighting of the living room. Clean metal, metal that had not yet been tarnished. As if it never been used to smack his sister in the head.

I dreamed that. I dreamed all of it.

Am I dreaming now?

A shrill scream severed him from his thoughts. He knew where it had come from. Over the dunes and down the beach, where he noticed a significant amount of orange, flickering light.

From where he heard the whispers.

FIFTEEN

The sight before him was too surreal—twelve figures stood clad in dark robes, hoods hiked over their heads, concealing their identities, and Garrett thought that was for the best. Easier on his conscience, easier to do what needed to be done. It'd be much harder if he had to *see* the faces he was smashing in. It would make the experience much more human.

Garrett stormed down the dunes and spotted his sister immediately. In the center of the torch-lit circle, a long wooden box shaped like a casket rested atop a stone altar. Jean was next to it, her hand combing over the casket's smooth, sanded exterior, as if she were getting acquainted with the material, the way one might inspect a future purchase. Then she turned and glanced over in his direction. Her eyes were alarming. The one eye that belonged to her remained as it had been, but the contrast of the eye owned by that invading presence gave Garrett some pause. It seemed to glow in the darkness iridescently, a lustrous display of milky prisms.

That wasn't the only alarming thing about what Garrett saw of Jean. In fact, her new eye was her least unsettling feature.

What disturbed him the most was the scaly patches that covered her arms, legs, and neck. A dark spot of fish skin was layered over her now misshapen forehead.

This was not his sister. Not anymore.

He stood there frozen for a few beats, his brain trying to process the images before him, trying to make sense of it all. But there was no making sense of this madness, and Garrett teetered on the brink of that other side, that space between two worlds where madness and reality coexisted. He blinked several times, attempting to free his mind of what could only be a grand illusion conjured by Tripp's Isle's magical interference. But his mind would not let go of them. The world remained unchanged.

"Garrett," Patti said to him, seemingly delighted by his presence. He could tell her jubilance was an act; she was annoyed by his return.

Leave.

That had been her. She'd left him that note. As well as the smelly dark fish eggs back on that first night. *Fresh catch.* Now that she was here before him, playing out her part in the madness that turned Jean into that other *thing*, he knew Patti was responsible for a lot more, maybe *everything*.

Maybe his uncle's death.

"Jean," Garrett said, gripping the hammer's handle tightly with both hands. "Come here."

Jean didn't move.

"She doesn't belong to you anymore, Garrett," said Patti's husband, *Peter*. His slick smile revealed bloated gums and cracked teeth, dark stains starting at the roots and working their way up. Even in the moonlight, Garrett could see they were in advanced stages of rot. "She's in our care now. We promise we will protect her."

"Whatever this is," Garrett said, pointing the hammer at him, "it ends now. All of it."

"And if it doesn't?" Peter's chest swelled with pride. The old man folded his arms defiantly. "What will you do? You're not exactly a threat, Garrett. Not to all fourteen of us." He glanced over his shoulder at Jean. "Fifteen," he corrected.

"It ends. *Now*." Garrett stood his ground. There was no turning back. No time for cowardice.

"When did you grow a spine, boy?" Patti said, chuckling under her breath.

"Fuck you, lady."

"Enough of his nonsense," Peter said, waving his hand dismissively. He turned the corner of his mouth to his right shoulder and said, "Get him."

Two of the closest robed figures marched forward. Garrett readied the hammer in his hands. Patti and Peter turned their backs on the situation, considering the thing handled.

Garrett intended to disappoint them.

The robed figures charged forward, and Garrett swung for the fences.

———

A LITTLE GIRL wearing a wreath on her head held Jean's hand. Together, they studied the casket. Though, *tomb* was more accurate.

"I know it's scary," said the little girl. "But you are strong."

"Why do I have to?" Jean asked, keeping her voice as even as she could considering the circumstance.

The little girl squeezed her hand. It was a nice, soft gesture, but it did nothing to ease Jean's discomfort.

"It's part of the deal," the little girl said, and when Jean studied her face, she understood the little girl was *her*, the six-year-old version of Jean Pryce. The little girl who was more of a tomboy than a little girl, the little girl who had always wanted to play football or street hockey with her brother and the neighborhood boys. The little girl who was a daddy's girl up until his earthly exit.

"What deal?"

"Tripp's Isle's deal." The little girl faced the men clad in dark robes and the one white-robed fiend that was responsible for this whole mess. "They want to communicate with the other side, but they don't have any idea what they're doing. They think if they hand us over to the other side, that *other* world, that the void will return something magnificent. An exchange."

"What will it do?" Jean asked, fearing the answer.

The little girl smirked, then rested her head against Jean's hip affectionately. She cooed. "Oh, it will only spare their lives. For a little while. Their end is inevitable."

"What does that mean?"

The girl's two iridescent eyes beamed in the torchlit night. The sinister gaze caused Jean's skin to come crawling alive. "Means this place is coming to an end. That the sea and the stars will swallow the shore, and the people of this place will fall into the depths of the void, to be eaten and digested by the great mouth of time."

Not the answer Jean was expecting, but she nodded like she understood what it all meant. "I don't want to go." She was on the verge of tears. The little girl hugged her tighter.

"You have to. I will keep you safe on the other side. I am your conveyer."

Jean glanced down to see the little girl's body melting into her hip, as if their two bodies had been conjoined at birth. The little girl's face from her nose down had sunken into her, the fabric of her shorts becoming one with her flesh. Her skin stretched like melted taffy. Those warping eyes continued to peer up at her, evil yet somehow still conveying a touch of innocence.

"I am one with you," the little girl's voice called, impressive considering her mouth was now inside Jean's body, absorbed by the liquid properties of this clear illusion. She didn't sound like a little girl anymore, either. Her voice was deep and dark and raspy like a busy nest of vexed wasps. *"We are one with the sea, the stars."*

The girl's elastic face fused into Jean's body, and a heavenly glow filled Jean's heart. Her final breath was near and she was hardly ready for it, but like all things, there was no escaping what awaited at the end of life's torturous journey.

There was no escaping the endless sea and the infinite stars.

THE Y MOVED FASTER than Garrett had expected. He thought the robes would hinder their movement, but he was wrong. They moved like apparitions in mid-haunt, slithering through the pale shadows, dipping and sliding toward their one and only goal; to capture Garrett and end whatever disruptions he could potentially cause.

But Garrett wouldn't give himself over, not easily. He'd never been a fit kid—his sister was always the athletic one—and had never seen the inside of a gym in his adult life, so he doubted he had the ability to match up against any single one of these mysterious robed brutes, let alone all twelve of them. But he'd certainly try.

What he lacked in physicality, he'd make up with rage and a brand-new appetite for violence.

The first cult member came at him with outstretched arms. Garrett aimed for the figure's center, knocking the fool right on the hood. He brought the hammer down with force and listening to the wet smack that followed was almost enough to make him squeal with delight. It felt good unleashing all that rage in a single, focused act. The robed human—at least, he assumed they were human—stumbled a bit before staggering to one knee. Once his opponent was felled, Garrett took the opportunity to deliver the knockout blow. He brought the hammer down on the crown of their head with such force that the muscles in both arms ached from the contact. The crunch that followed echoed throughout the silent night.

Oh shit, he thought, watching the figure go limp, then fall forward like some tree severed from the base of its trunk. The figure hit the sand and did not move. A dark fluid leaked through the robe's fabric, staining the dim beach sand beneath it.

The second approaching figure stopped to inspect what had just happened, and the figure seemed to hesitate, perhaps to rethink their strategy or the attack altogether. Garrett decided it was best not to allow the bastard any time to second guess their decision. He lunged forward and screamed, a ferocious war cry that filled the night, echoing across the beach and stretching over the small black waves that crashed on the dusky shoreline. The robed figure continued to deliberate, and their inability to make a decision cost them. Garrett struck the figure on the hood, breaking the skin and bone hidden beneath it. The figure went stumbling back three or four steps before the strength in their legs gave out, sending them sprawling across the sand. They tried to recover but Garrett was on them, continuously swinging the hammer against the black sheet that covered their human form. Screams and the sweet sounds of bones breaking in multiple spots gave Garrett the knowledge that these were indeed humans beneath the garments. The blood that soaked through the fabric was further evidence.

Garrett stopped swinging when the body ceased fighting and started twitching. Then he focused on his next target. Five of the ten figures were coming after him, each running to meet their adversary.

He readied the hammer. Then got to work.

SHE LAY in the box and gazed lazily at the stars. Some of them blinked like cosmic eyes. Some were different colors, lit with greenish and bluish tints. An aurora of greenish-blue light, a celestial streak that looked like someone had stepped on the stars and shoe-dragged them across a concrete sky, paraded laterally across the darkened airspace, slow like sap moving along a gradual decline. Watching this lesson in astronomy brought peace to her mind, filling her with unparalleled seren-ity. She felt like she was floating across the cosmos, weaving between the stars herself, as if she were one with the drifting aurora.

Then she realized she *was* moving. The whole box was. She glanced around and saw five of the robed figures escorting her toward the ocean. The waves clapping against the shore grew louder. The briny tang of the foamy surf overpowered her sense of smell. Within seconds, there was liquid all around her and she was floating. A lid went over the box, and then there was nothing but darkness, water, and the realization that she was going to fall asleep and never wake up again.

But she didn't fear death.

The thing inside her—that passenger of some alternate perdition—told her this was not the end but the beginning, that a new life was waiting for her on the other side, one free of pain and sacrifice and the typical taxations exclusive to human suffering.

The being born from that other side told her this and so much more.

And she bought every word of it.

GARRETT SWIPED the hammer at the closest figure and the figure backed away, causing Garrett to miss by mere inches. The five enemies formed a circle around him, each representing a point on the pentagram-shaped alignment. They were evenly distanced from him, just out of reach of his hammer's danger zone.

"We rush him at the same time," one of them said, and Garrett could hear the frustration and hostility in that voice. "He can't attack us all at once."

The others shortened the distance with a few steps.

Garrett didn't wait for them to put the plan in motion. He went for the one that had spoken the plan out loud, thrusting his dominant arm forward, propelling the hammer at his desired target. The face of the hammer came down flush, and Garrett felt the bone splinter beneath its momentum. The figure dropped to the ground without restraint. Garrett got the hammer back into a full swing but was only able to connect with one more target before arms were on him, all around him, wrestling him away from making further contact. In the chaos that unfolded before him, the flurry of robed limbs and undulating fabric, Garrett saw a flash of metal glint before him, and it did not come from the hammer in his hand. Pain exploded through his midsection, cutting him deep. His mind was immediately alert, knowing something dangerous had happened, possibly deadly. He saw one of the figures holding a knife, the blade being withdrawn from his abdomen. The knife was thrust back into him, and the figure repeated this movement three, four more times. Splashes of blood exited him with each stab. An arm went under his chin and pulled back, hard, causing his spine to arch in the most unnatural way. He heard a sharp crack, felt a panic-inducing numbness, and the first thought that entered his mind was *my spine is broken*. The world suddenly went silent, and his limbs felt weightless. He lay there on top of the figure who was choking him, waiting for death to take him, whisk him away to that place where the outer dark covered everything, where there was no sight or sound or anything save for the impenetrable shadows, dense and eternal.

He waited for that special darkness to claim his vision, but it didn't come.

As the blade came down a sixth time, he was suddenly inspired to give it one last effort, one last chance to save himself, his sister, and get out of Tripp's Isle alive.

He dipped to the side, managing to avoid the blade's sharp movement. The figure with their hands around Garret's throat let out an audible gasp. The blade had missed Garrett and disappeared into the figure's midsection. The choker eased up just enough for Garrett to break free. Once he did, he felt the others grab onto him, their fingers gripping his arms, digging in. Garrett swung his fists wildly, driving his knuckles into their faces, heaving as many punches as he could, which helped back them up a few feet. He turned over, facing the figure who'd been choking him, and drove the hammer into their face. The violent crunch ended them and any chance they'd have of recovering from the stabbing.

Next, Garrett got to his feet. It wasn't easy, and the ground rocked below him as if the sand were the tide reacting to an impending storm. One of the robed fiends pointed at him, an almost comical gesture that reminded him of a professional wrestler climbing into the ring and letting the crowd know that their mark was gonna get thrashed, but Garrett ignored his instinct to laugh and, instead, leapt forward with the hammer and struck them in the face. The others came at him, but he didn't care. He turned on his heels and began striking them with the hammer, so fast and fierce that the robed figures could not react in time. He punished one who lingered too close, smashing them over and over again in the neck region. One of the strikes landed across their jaw, and Garrett felt the bones shatter on impact. The robed figure's hands went to their broken jaw, and they stumbled away into the shroud of night, becoming one with the shadows, from where they would never return. One of the other figures he'd abused with the hammer turned around and ambled off in the opposite direction, up the dunes and away from the beach, abandoning their cultic duties.

That left Garrett with one more enemy from this first wave. He imagined the lone remaining member seething underneath that hood, which made what would come next all the sweeter. The figure cocked back their head and howled at the luminous moon. Then they charged, lowering their shoulder to spear Garrett, shoot him to the ground. But Garrett saw the move coming and was able to get the hammer on the back of what he perceived to be the figure's neck. The strike forced the figure to miss his shot. Garrett easily sidestepped the stumbling figure's attempt and watched as the robed body lost control of their legs and fell awkwardly to the sand. Garrett pounced on him, finishing him with three accurate chops on the back of his head. The sick sounds of splitting skin and a fissuring brainpan did not affect him. Nothing did anymore. Not even his own injuries, the ones that were currently leaking an alarming amount of blood down his front side.

Garrett swept the immediate area with his eyes. The figures on the ground weren't moving and the ones lucky enough to remain on their feet had defected.

He moved on.

Toward his new targets.

The man in black and the woman in the white robe.

SIXTEEN

"Do you hear that?" Peter said to his wife while watching five of his followers escort Jean Pryce's body toward the threshold between two realities. "It sounds like..."

"Screaming?" Patti said, turning to face the direction where the others were dealing with the evening's minor nuisance. Peter couldn't believe the bastard had come back, but surprises were a part of life, and if Peter had learned anything about life in his seventy years in this reality, it was always suspect the unexpected.

Later, he'd wish he had learned to *expect* the unexpected.

The screaming grew louder.

"What in the hell..." he said, turning around to meet the noise.

He saw Garrett Pryce emerge from the dimness, carrying an object over his head, arm cocked back like a pitcher gearing up for a ninety-mile-per-hour fastball.

"Oh no," was all Patti could get out before Garrett lunged forward and drove the hammer's bloodied head into the space above her eyes. Peter watched his wife's head dent on impact, fold in like a car door in a minor traffic accident. The force drove her off her feet, and she dropped to the sand immediately.

Rage fueled Peter's mouth. "You motherfucking piece of shit," he snapped, his face tightening with a level of anger he never knew he could ascend. "You rotten, cowardly fuck—"

No sooner than he could think of an appropriate reaction, the hammer's face was laid upon Peter's noggin.

The world exploded into a kaleidoscope of blurry stars. There were no more thoughts. Peter tried to hold onto what little light remained of the world. But when the second hammer-smash came for him, there was only darkness, and Peter knew nothing more of this reality, or the one he'd been searching for, for such a long, long time.

PATTI SAID SOMETHING, but to Garrett, it sounded like someone trying to pronounce the random letters that appeared in their alphabet soup. She was still alive; her husband—not so much. Garrett ensured he would not return to the land of the living. He'd taken the hammer to his skull several times until his flesh and brainpan came apart like the shell of a dropped egg. What rested above the man's neck was mostly clumps of mutilated brains and smashed bits of flesh and bloody bone broth.

Garrett leaned over Patti. He grabbed her by the hair. Blood leaked from a nose that was now sitting slightly askew, two dark streams that poured into the shadows beneath her. The woman's eyes glazed back. She was on the verge of trespassing into the eternal realm that awaited her, but Garrett wanted to send her off the right way.

"Fuck you, Patti," he said, then brought the hammer down

as hard as he could on the center of her forehead. Again and again. Until every feature on her face was resting in a spot it never had before, forever rearranged.

———

GARRETT LET OUT one high-energy battle cry, so the five figures hip-deep in the ocean's shallows knew he was coming. Then, like a soldier given permission to attack the opposing first line, he charged forth into battle.

The five figures looked to each other, obviously not expecting this to be a part of whatever ceremony they'd come here to perform. One of them must have seen the condition of their leaders, because when Garrett neared the wet sand where the surf washed up, they let go of the casket and took off sideways, keeping a wide berth from their potential attacker.

Garrett let them go. He was only interested in the casket, saving his sister. The first robe he went after put up their arm, as if that was going to block the strike. It didn't, and the action resulted in a fractured forearm; Garrett heard the snap when the hammer connected. The next strike went into the side of their head, dropping the figure in the shallow water. They landed face down with a *plop!*, and Garrett wished with every fiber in his body that the figure would drown on their own, without having to waste precious time drowning them himself. He knocked the felled figure on the back of the head once more for insurance.

The remaining figures seemed confused about what to do next. One of them followed his brethren and took off, paddling in the opposite direction, back toward the beach.

Let them go, let them all go.

One of the others put up their hands and pleaded. "Please, I don't—"

Garrett answered by clubbing him in the mouth. An awful snap followed, and the figure's hands went to where the damage had been done. A terrible scream erupted, and Garrett silenced them at once with a follow-up, slugging the figure in the side of the head. Seconds later, the robe and the body it covered went floating in the direction of the sea, that invisible threshold between two open worlds.

The last remaining member made the smart decision to abandon the effort, diving for the shore, pumping their arms and legs so rapidly that they made it to the shoreline in about five seconds flat.

Garrett was alone with the wooden box now, the one that contained his sister. His heart was pumping so fast that he felt lightheaded. He screamed one more time, a primal sound that announced to all of Tripp's Isle that he was victorious. He had won. The people of this place had lost. And his sister was safe.

She's safe. With me, she always will be.

He lugged the wooden box back to shore, dragged it up the beach. Opened it. Inside, his sister rested. Eyes open. Staring up at the stars, the conch resting in both hands. Her pale flesh looked bluish beneath the moon's luminous touch.

"Oh, Jean..." he said, brushing back the loose, wet hair that clung to her cold face.

In the shallows, Garrett watched a dark figure—one that looked a little too much like his sister—step backwards in the surf, wading until its different colored eyes were swallowed up by the tide, until it disappeared and became one with the inky waters.

Garrett sat on the beach alone with the sea and the stars as the whispers of this place faded and, eventually, died, becoming nothing but a distant memory of this endless, silent evening.

"On the faraway shores of that strange world, the eyes watched from the distant hollows of the cosmos and the unimaginable depths of the black sea."

– Garrett Pryce, *The Sea, the Stars*

THE END

ABOUT THE AUTHOR

Tim Meyer dwells in a dark cave near the Jersey Shore. He's written and published over fifteen novels and novellas, including Malignant Summer, The Switch House, Dead Daughters, Limbs, and many other titles. His screenplay adaptation for The Switch House has won two finalist awards (Semifinalist, ScreenCraft Horror Competition 2020 & Semifinalist, Filmmatic Horror Screenplay Awards 5). He exists on coffee and IPAs.

You can visit him at timmeyerwrites.com.

Lightning Source UK Ltd.
Milton Keynes UK
UKHW010904201022
410800UK00005B/580